A series of B-52s strafed the flaming hillside ...

with water, specially treated with detergents to increase its wetness. At the edges of the billowing cloud that rose above the blaze, an eddy of smoke detached from the greater mass and huddled in upon itself.

The creature was dark at first, visible only in silhouette against the landscape, but its color changed as the particles within it began to rage. Hints of green and gold changed to violet. For an instant it became canary yellow in a flash of sodium luminescence. Then its entire form took on an orange and violet sheen.

It sped after a B-52 and made short work of the aircraft. A few light touches and the wings took fire, aluminum alloy exploding into the searing incandescence of a thermite bomb. Then the plane exploded, the water cargo flashing into steam.

The creature leaped upon the hot blue cloud and consumed it. All who watched heard it. The scream of mockery lingered until, with a final, laughing cry, it merged with the dark smog clouds overhead.

JAMES KILLUS
SUNSMOKE

ACE SCIENCE FICTION BOOKS
NEW YORK

SUNSMOKE

An Ace Science Fiction Book / published by arrangement with
the author

PRINTING HISTORY
Ace Original / March 1985

ISBN: 0-441-79083-6

Ace Science Fiction Books are published by
The Berkley Publishing Group,
200 Madison Avenue, New York, New York 10016.
PRINTED IN THE UNITED STATES OF AMERICA

To the memory of Steve Sasaki,
who taught many things
that I needed to know.

PART ONE

I LOVE L.A.

Prologue

The pentagram on the CRT cast phosphor green light into the room, and made his face look sickly and gaunt. The only other illumination was provided by the scented candle which perched upon the fossil skull in the corner. The only sounds came from the rattle of coins in the small refrigerator and the occasional hiss of the coffee pot.

He arose abruptly, his movements jerky and agitated. He yawned and stretched, then shook himself convulsively. He stepped over to the refrigerator and opened it. It was nearly barren, but he found a candy bar in the freezer. He unwrapped it, crammed several mouthfuls down his throat, then washed it down with bitter coffee. He opened a vial of amphetamines from his pocket, took three, and washed those down with coffee also.

He returned to the terminal, sat down, and began to type.

```
EXECUTION TRACE:   SMOGMOD IV
FAST FOURIER ADAPTIVE CYCLE TECHNIQUE
PARAMETER SEARCH:   STOICHIOMETRY

   RUN#   RESULT
   1A     INVALID MASS BALANCE:   CARBON
   1B     INVALID  MASS  BALANCE:  UNPAIRED
          OXYGEN
   2A     NEGATIVE            CONCENTRATION
          DETECTED
   2B     IN EXECUTION
```

Run 2B finished as he watched. These things were taking too long and not leading in the direction he'd hoped. He sighed. Maybe this next trick would work. He typed:

```
ADDON CHECKFFACT
RECYCLE:
EXECUTE
```

For a moment his hands felt sticky, as if someone had spilled warm syrup on the keyboard. He looked at his hands and was briefly startled to see them covered with blood. Then he realized that the sun had risen and that, to his CRT-bleary eyes, everything seemed red in the dawning light. He hit RETURN.

The pain in his chest came suddenly, giving him no chance to cry out. He died immediately, slumping forward so that his hands pushed forward into the scarlet morning light.

The day was June 6. It was six A.M. The monster's birth had no living witness.

Tuesday Morning: Peters

When Peters arrived at Shreiber Manse, Arthur and Beth had just finished taking apart the Rubik Cube. Matthew was arguing that it should be possible (with the proper application of a hacksaw that he happened to have with him) to make a Soma set out of the pieces. Arthur was willing to try it, but it was Beth's cube and Beth was dubious.

"Wally!" called out Doug Shreiber, Proprietor of the Manse, as he was sometimes labeled, half in jest, half in irony. "Get your ass over here and have some drugs!"

Peters winced slightly. He did not like nicknames,

especially "Wally," and he knew that Shreiber did it just to annoy him. Shreiber did a lot of things just to be annoying. But Peters did not let his annoyance keep him from padding over to the enormous sofa and accepting a toke from the giant brass waterpipe.

"Maybe just a little bit," he said in that strained voice that is used when trying to keep smoke from interfering with speech. "I'm down here on business, and besides, as you know, my interest in these things is purely scientific."

"Bullshit," said Monica, sweeping her leg underneath Peters in a judo maneuver which deposited him next to her on the sofa. She then kissed him, mightily, managing to pull the last dregs of smoke from his mouth into hers. "Yummy," she said. "Dougie filled the waterpipe with rose petals and spearmint. Dougie knows how to show his guests a good time." She grinned as impishly as is possible for a woman nearly six feet tall. Shreiber tried not to show any reaction to her use of "Dougie."

"We're just about to break out the nitrous tank," said Shreiber. "Want some?" He looked at Peters.

"Yes, but I can't. Honestly. Much as I would like to join you folks in your debauchery, I really am down here on business and I have to be straight for this afternoon."

"What's up?"

"Bugs in one of our models. It's the same thing that brought me down here the last time. We've been trying for a couple of years now to do real-time simulations of the Los Angeles airshed: put all the data collection on phone lines, feed the whole thing into an adaptive model, then just sit back and watch the thing tell you what's going on in the wonderful world of smog. That's the intent, anyway. It was going great until last week. Then predictions and observations began to diverge. So they called on Mr. Wonderful—that's me—to come down and bail them out. I was planning on a trip down anyway so this works out just fine.''

"How long will you be staying?" asked Monica. "Do you need a place to crash?"

"Length of stay: indeterminate. Probably a week or two. As for sleeping accommodations, I am open to suggestions. Propositions, too, but later. This afternoon is for business and I have to be up early tomorrow to get to a funeral.''

"Funeral?" inquired Shreiber

"Yeah, a colleague of mine. You probably don't remember him. Fellow named Raymond Macgregor. He died of a heart attack last Wednesday.''

"How old was he?"

"Thirty-four."

"Jeez, that's young for it," opined Monica.

"Young enough," said Shreiber. "When you have a heart attack that young you usually die from it. It's only old people who survive."

Peters shrugged. "He was a fitness-type to boot. He studied the martial arts, too." He looked at Monica. "Karate," he said. "Big muscles. Maybe he was overtrained.''

Several other people had wandered over to the waterpipe. One of them was Larry, who used to draw comics before he had taken up semipermanent residence in the Manse. Larry paused before taking another hit.

"Was there anything else to it? What drugs did he like, for example?" Larry asked.

"I honestly don't know," said Peters. "I didn't know him that well, actually. We were both in school together for a little while. I knew his wife better than I knew him; I dated her before she met Ray. He came on the scene the year I left, a transfer student from Australia. Smart. Ambitious. Hard to get to know. Martian cyborg-type. The sort that won't give you a reaction until they've consulted homebase.''

"Let me guess," said Monica. "You didn't like him."

"You've found me out," said Peters. "But don't make too big a deal of it. I don't like a lot of people —present company excepted."

Then he kissed her again.

Shreiber Manse was a permanent party open to all who could meet the rigorous membership requirement: the ability to keep Doug Shreiber amused. The Manse had a swimming pool and a Jacuzzi and wet and dry saunas. It had a tennis court and a billiard room. It had a still in the basement and a greenhouse on the roof that managed to supply most of the party's requirements of marijuana, peyote, and morning-glory seeds. Narcotics were verboten, which is to say that one could indulge in them if one were not too obvious. Shreiber found junkies a bore. Also he was a devout believer in the laws of karma. "Whenever you buy cocaine or heroin," he had once said, "you are, at most, two people away from a man with a gun. Giving money to people with guns is a bad habit and should be avoided whenever possible." Whenever one of his libertarian friends used a statement like this to bring up arguments against the income tax, Shreiber would note that all of *his* money was in tax-free bonds and would then change the subject.

None of which prevented Shreiber from having twice tried unsuccessfully to grow coca in his greenhouse. And opium poppies had been seen there from time to time.

Shreiber was a bio-mathematician who had made his fortune in the commodities market using a trend-seeking algorithm based on the random-search patterns of amoebae. He'd gotten out when other traders began playing the same game, to the detriment of his payoff margin. Besides, he had enough money to support his intended lifestyle.

Shreiber's friends were a wide cross section of artists, intellectuals, and beautiful women. Occasionally all three attributes would be combined in one individual, as was the case with Monica, his former wife.

Monica had an athlete's body, large boned and over six-feet tall in high heels, which she seldom wore. She had dark curly hair and high cheekbones that hinted of a mixture of Latin and Asian ancestry some generations back. She was a native Californian, but she had attended schools in the East, finishing with a spell at Columbia. Her time in the Big Apple had revved her wits a bit, and she could outtalk most New Yorkers, if provoked. Her sarcasm was legendary.

She was a fair artist, a clever photographer and, by her own admission, a mediocre writer. After returning to Los Angeles from New York, she had spent some time in local repertory theater and had made several movies, none of them memorable. She had also made several directors, one of whom she married.

When Doug Shreiber met her, he immediately decided that she was what he had been looking for since he had made his first million. At the time, both he and she were married, though not to each other. They soon rectified both situations. It then took them about two years to realize that they could not stand both living together and being married to each other. Since they still both loved, wanted, and needed each other, they got divorced. His second, her fourth.

Their marriage had been a simple ceremony; their divorce was the occasion for one of the biggest parties to ever exist outside of a press agent's imagination. It had yet to end. Peters's only quarrel with the setup was that he could never remember anyone's last name.

The Monster

The newborn slept, cradled on the hot layers of the city's desert air. Its metabolism was, for now, benign, even beneficial. It inhaled the fumes of civilization and gave back pristine purity. Its cell structure gorged on the toxins. It grew fat and dense with its future purpose.

Its dreams were at first without form, hard edges merely, that cleaved the dark spaces of a place that was not a place. But the jagged patterns found joinings and small furies formed. Vengeful dreams sputtered and twitched.

The monster turned gently in its sleep, basking in the sun. As it turned, little shards drifted from its dreamspace. Hot little snowflakes ready to live, ready to become real.

Tuesday Afternoon: Peters

Peters arrived at the research office for the South Coast Air Quality Management District a little after lunch. He had taken a leisurely drive out the San Bernardino Freeway before turning south toward the El Monte offices of SCAQMD (pronounced "Squaw mud" by friend and foe alike). The day was pleasant, the air surprisingly clear; the smell of late spring blooms masked any smell of smog.

"Your model is really screwing up," said Mei Lin Liu as he walked into her office.

As he sat down he tried batting his eyes at her, asking, "Why is it when it screws up it's my model and when it works, it's *our* model?" She laughed.

"Well," she said, "*our* model is really screwing up. It says that today should be a stage-one advisory. Instead, it's cleaner than it has been for weeks. That's the way it's gone for about a week now. The model has been predicting light to moderate, but we've had a clearing trend."

"What do the meteorologists say?" he asked.

"I don't know, I haven't asked. Maybe Bob knows."

Bob didn't know. Neither did Ann or Barry. In fact it turned out that no one in the modeling group had asked any of the meteorologists about the smog level. This was probably because the meteorology group had moved to a new building several months before, and the new telephone switchboard tended to lose calls. It would be fixed "real soon now" but as a result, all accidental, informal communication between the two groups had ceased. No water-cooler gossip, no chance encounters in the hall. No one was sure who had the responsibility for formal communication.

"Well hell," said Peters. "I don't do it in the dark. My first rule of simulation modeling is, 'Never try to find an answer until you know what one looks like.' Call up your Met guys and let them know I'm coming."

Twenty minutes later he was in the office of Paul Duckworth, meteorologist for the California Air Resources Board, temporarily on loan to SCAQMD. "We've got a problem," Peters told Duckworth. "The model says smoggy but the nose, eyes, and throat say clear. To be more precise, peak ozone today should be somewhere in the vicinity of Upland, reaching a maximum concentration of about a quarter of a part per million. The monitors perversely persist in measuring ozone below the national ambient air quality standard of twelve parts per hundred million. Are there any meteorological factors which are unusual? Just what gives, huh?'' For some reason, Peters was beginning to feel a bit punchy.

Duckworth's answer was no help. ''No,'' he said. ''Met factors are quite ordinary. Winds are light to moderate. Delta T through the inversion is about two degrees, the temperature aloft is twenty-six degrees Centigrade. Everything that we know about the Los Angeles microclimate points to this being an ordinary, typical, run-of-the-mill stage-one advisory smog day.'' He paused and smiled. ''Hell, if you can't believe your meteorologist, who can you trust?'' Peters stared at him dumbly.

''Oh yeah,'' said Duckworth. ''If you think today is bad, wait till tomorrow. A high-pressure cell is stabilizing. Tomorrow should be a real killer.''

```
EXECUTION TRACE:   SMOGMOD IV
      LAGRANGIAN PUFF SUBMODEL
LOCATION:   40587.23, 1548.03 UTM COORDINATES
CELL (1.78,22.47)
          X       Y
TIME:   18:43:17
AVERAGE CONCENTRATIONS (PPM)
O₃              0.03
NO              0.001
NO₂             0.008
OLEFIN          0.21
PARAFFIN        1.45
ETHENE          0.26
AROMATIC        0.35
CO              57802O.2
H₂O₂            0.0002
HNO₂            0.0001
HNO₃            0.002
RADICAL CONCENTRATIONS NOT FILED
```

Tuesday Afternoon: Alan

"Nice day for a walk, eh Sadie?" Alan asked. He expected no reply, not even a bark. But Sadie reversed herself twice, not really *trying* to get both of them tangled up in her leash—he doubted that she had the brains for that—but just out of high-spirited clumsiness.

Nimbly avoiding the leash trap, he reached down and gave her a few energetic pats. "You're a dumb blonde, Sadie, but I love you." She bounded away and nearly took his arm off before he managed to break into a run himself.

Sadie was a champagne-colored afghan hound, and it was with only a faint touch of owner's pride that he considered her to be the most beautiful dog he'd ever seen. As he'd once remarked to a friend, you know you really have something when people come out of their houses to say "What a beautiful dog!" while she's shitting on their front lawn.

She was friendly too, an all-around pleasant animal to own. But dumb? Dumb! He sometimes joked that she was too dumb to remember which leg to raise.

She stopped suddenly, cutting across his path again (*of course*, but he was used to her tricks) to examine a curbstone for obvious odors. He stood there breathing heavily, and reminded himself that it was time to start getting back into shape. Too much deskwork and not enough racketball was his diagnosis. Maybe he'd start riding his bike to work again. Especially if this nice weather held up. . . .

Sadie suddenly looked up with a startled expression on her face. She shook her head once and then lit out again. He tried to keep up with her, to not pull back so much on the leash. But she was really straining at it and he was suddenly very tired. And there was this smell of car exhaust, although the street was empty. The air smelled sort of stale.

He coughed and Sadie pulled the leash out of his hand. "Sadie!" he yelled after her, as he stumbled and almost fell. He righted himself and grabbed onto a streetlamp. The air didn't smell like exhaust anymore, but it wasn't fresh air either. He realized that he was going to be sick.

He retched, trying not to soil himself. There was a hammering in his head. The light seemed to dim, like a cloud passing in front of the sun. The street was still deserted, but from somewhere a voice seemed to say, "What a beautiful man!" as he threw up on someone's front lawn and passed out.

Peters

Sunset found Peters still staring bleary-eyed into a CRT, searching for, if not answers, at least a few good questions. He lost track of time. When he finally noticed that he had been hungry for hours, he sent out for food. He barely noticed when it arrived.

He searched for anomalies. What was it about the past few days that was different? What had happened to the smog?

Ozone, the principal component of smog, was very low in concentration at most monitoring sites. Near background. Visibility, as measured by light scattering nephelometers, was likewise unimpaired. Well, okay. There is no smog because it isn't there. Clear enough?

The two main smog precursors, reactive hydrocarbon and nitrogen oxide, were still present, however. So people still drove their cars and fueled them with gasoline. It was nice to know that something still happened as it should.

There was something odd about the RHC and NO_x

measurements though. Normally the measured ratios of RHC and NO_x were about five or six to one in the west near the coast because the photochemical process destroys NO_x faster than hydrocarbons; the ratio increased moving east, with the wind, away from the coast.

Today, though, some of the measurements looked screwy. The *average* ratios were about the same as they'd always been. But if he broke them down into smaller time periods, the ratios looked anomalous. A RHC/NO_x ratio of one hundred to one would be followed by a ratio of 0.1 to 1. And carbon monoxide looked a bit funny too.

It had to be bad data. Either that or someone had loosed Maxwell's demon on L.A., instructed to carefully pile up all the molecules of hydrocarbon over here, and nitric oxide over there, so they couldn't mix, couldn't react to form smog.

He sighed, got up and put on his hat. When you start having crazy ideas like that, it's time to go home.

Tuesday Evening: Williams

It was a nothing bar, but then, in his opinion, Bakersfield had always been a nothing town. Usually he just shot straight on through to L.A. but right now he needed a couple of beers to take the edge off the amphetamine jangle that he'd let himself in for. Goddamn it, they'd looked like real black beauties when he'd bought them, but they'd turned out to have some sort of homebrew crank in them instead, and were not smooth or even.

They did the job though. And when you had to keep a rig on the road for thirty-six hours straight, well, anything that worked was better than nothing at all.

"Can we get wrestling on the box tonight?" Some San Joaquin Valley hick was trying to get the big-time stuff from L.A.

The bartender said, "Probably not. The missus likes it, but we can only get it maybe two nights out of five at home. And we have a big antenna there."

"Give her a try anyhow. Can't hurt to try." Alcohol makes for optimism.

The barkeep ran his hand down the remote control and after a few flashes of static, the picture cleared. Some guy with a multicolored mohawk was drop kicking a blond guy with about twelve tattoos.

"Hey, all right!" said the wrestling fanatic.

"Picture's real sharp tonight, considering," said the bartender. "Must be an inversion."

"In what?"

"Inversion. I don't know exactly, but they call them inversions. Layers in the air. Radio and TV bounces around for a while and sometimes if things are just right, they hop over the mountains and come out here. We could lose the signal any time."

The picture cut to a commercial. One of the drunks blew a raspberry.

"Hey," said the bartender. "You gotta take the good with the bad.

Williams grimaced into his beer and tried to ignore it all. Jesus, what a dump. High-class highlights from nowhere. Bullshit wrestling. Maybe he should have just bought a six-pack and drunk it in the cab, and to hell with the rules.

Then suddenly, there were Colby and Trina on the TV. In the middle of some pizza commercial.

"Hey!" he shouted. "Those are my kids!"

Heads turned to look at him.

He lowered his voice, but he couldn't stop from

continuing. "My kids. Goddamn it! You think I don't know 'em? That's Colby and Trina. What are they doing on TV?"

"Making money, most likely," came the retort and everybody thought that was real funny.

Peters

Peters did not return to the Manse until past midnight. Shreiber had retired to bed and the party had begun to dissipate. There came soft splashes from the pool area. Occasionally quiet laughter spilled from the sixties nostalgia room. Peters poked his head into the blacklit cubbyhole and almost broke into laughter himself. They'd added a big lava lamp since his last visit. From the stereo issued the voice of Ken Nordine extolling the virtues of Miss Cone.

He found Monica painting in her basement studio.

"More green," he told her. The painting was a black and white abstract.

"Hello Walter," she said, not looking up. She continued to fill in a black stripe. "You can't have been working this late. Where have you been?"

"I am a complex and complicated man," he said in a mildly ironic voice. "I violate tradition. I was indeed working."

"No!" she said in a mix of mock and real astonishment.

He shrugged. "I got into the notion of repeatedly banging my head into a brick wall."

"Ah," she said. "You got stubborn."

"Yeah, and I also lost track of time."

"Did you eat?" She reached for a new brush.

"Take-out pizza. I don't remember a bite."

She looked at him directly for the first time. "That's a bit obsessive, yes? Addict behavior?"

He grinned. "It's either work or laughing gas. I'm not cut out for the French Foreign Legion."

She gave a little half laugh and turned back to the painting. "Girl trouble," she said. "He works to forget."

He stepped back and looked around. "You know, if you moved the black lamps from the hippie room down here, you could probably generate some smog with all the solvent fumes. There might not be sufficient nitrogen oxides, though. You might have to burn some candles or incense. No, better still, a glass-blowing shop, lots of hot glass. Or a pottery kiln."

"One of the things that I love in you, Walter," she said, still working paint onto the canvas, "is the cleverness of your evasions. I always knew when you were unfaithful to me. You'd become almost too witty to bear."

She glanced at him. "But before you say something totally ludicrous about how you were always faithful to another man's wife, let me point out that you are dying to tell me of your most recent heartache and I am willing to coax you a bit. So what's her name?"

He sighed, as if to say you win, I'm tired and you were always better at this game anyway.

"Roberta," he said.

"What was her problem?"

"What do you mean?"

"You specialize in emotional basket cases, Walter. It's not like we haven't had this conversation before."

"I do not date only neurotics."

"No, but they are the only ones who get to you. Intelligent, creative, energetic neurotics. Where did you meet Roberta?"

"In the Oakland Airport parking lot. No wait, it's not as sordid as it sounds. She and I were on both halves of a round trip L.A. shuttle. I didn't sit with her but I noticed her. On the way out to the parking lot I asked her about her trip; it was a job interview. We talked for a while. She was an engineerng grad student at Cal. I called her up a few days later.''

"She gave you her number?''

"Her last name. I looked her up in the phone book.''

"Pretty brazen.''

"She got off on that, I think. I invited her to a Buster Keaton movie. She said yes, then called back an hour later to break the date. Something about too much work and neglecting friends and it wouldn't be right. I didn't try to change her mind although I'm pretty sure I could have.''

"An unusual application of good judgment,'' Monica said. The painting was nearly done.

He shrugged. "I said to myself, Peters, this one is too crazy, let her be.''

"So why didn't you?''

"Fate, I guess. Synchronicity. I ran into her the next day in the Cafe Med. We shared a table, had lunch together. Then we went for a walk in the park that turned into a hike in the hills.''

"So you seduced her.''

"I am no good at seduction.''

She shook her head and lay down the brush. The painting was complete. She turned to him.

"You mean you are no good at making passes. You can't handle the responsibility. But you are the most seductive man I've ever known. When you lived here you seduced everybody in the goddamn house.''

"Hey, I . . .''

"You know what I mean. You talked econometrics to Doug, and you did parapsychology experiments with Larry. You let Arthur teach you Kendo. You bought all the kids comics and windup toys and you spent hours taking the toys apart and showing the kids how they worked. Then you helped me commit adultery.''

"I meant no harm."

"I know . . . so what happened with Roberta?"

He touched his hand to his brow. "She had thick armor and a wild streak that frightened her. She was also non-orgasmic at first. In fact much of sex was painful to her. Tension and fear from a past trauma that I will not speak about."

"So you wanted to help."

"Oh yeah. That's me. God's gift to women. Just let Dr. Walt take care of you. Easy does it, no pressure from me."

"What was it you once told me? You balance your conceit with large doses of self-contempt?"

He made a rueful face. "Yeah, well, sex with Roberta slowly went from cautious and careful to energetic and fun. Then it got better than that, maybe even obsessive. Nearly mutual rape."

"Then she broke it off," Monica said.

He nodded. "It scared her. She told me that her father had been an alcoholic and she was afraid that she was showing the same sort of behavior, only about sex. Her grades slipped, not a lot, but enough to scare her."

"Poor Walter, he's so good in bed that it keeps losing him girl friends."

"Meow," he said flatly, like an old joke.

She touched his arm. "Did you love her? How does it feel to have her leave?"

"Sad. Wistful. Not too painful though. Not painful enough."

"So you're afraid that you didn't love her. That you were just using her? Guilt pangs maybe?"

"I meant no harm. I don't think that I *did* any harm. I think I even helped."

"But it wasn't love."

He gave her a tired smile. "Is it ever?"

"Sometimes one thinks so," she replied.

Wednesday Morning

Tomorrow should be a real killer.

The next day was glorious, clean and clear. The air smelled of sea breezes and honeysuckle. That's impossible, he thought. You haven't been near a honeysuckle vine since you left Tennessee.

"Nice day for a funeral," he said under his breath, as he got out of his car.

His head hurt, the way it always did when he came to Los Angeles. Before, he'd blamed the smog. That excuse taken from him, he blamed the long hours spent poring over wind and temperature data, and measurements from chemiluminescent detectors. He'd even brought some of the printouts back to Shreiber Manse with him, to Monica's further amazement.

The funeral party was small. Macgregor had little family in the United States. The group was made up of Macgregor's widow, Margaret, several friends, and some business associates. They made a sad little knot about the closed coffin.

"I'm glad you came," said Margaret. "It's good for me to have at least one friend here."

Peters shrugged. "I don't know what to say, Meg. It all seems kind of . . ." He stopped and shrugged again.

"Useless? Pointless? A waste? I'm sure it was all of that and more. I wish I knew more about it."

He looked at her quizzically.

"We separated over six months ago. You probably didn't hear." He shook his head. "I tried to write him off. Maybe I succeeded. I don't seem to feel much one way or the other, just sort of sad, like I wish it could have been different. I wish he could have been different.

"There was always such an air of excitement about Ray, you know? A hunger to him. It was pretty good when he was hungry for me, but not so good when it was his job, or a special project, or some other woman that he was wrapped up in."

He looked at her. "I never knew about any other women."

She bit her lip. "I'm not even sure of it myself. You hear things. You suspect things. You tell lies as easily as the truth when it's an argument. But he lost interest in me, I know that much. No more challenge to it; I was a game he'd won."

He felt a strong urge to hold her, to comfort her. *Going to console the widow*? his nasty little inner voice inquired. He fought down a mixture of conflicting impulses. Something of his struggle may have shown through. She grasped his arm.

"I know that the two of us wouldn't have worked any better than it worked with Ray. But at least if it had been the two of us it wouldn't have ended in a cemetery. Failure's bad enough without having to deal with death as well." She gave his arm one last convulsive clutch and then she turned and left.

He was still shaking his head slightly when a tall red-bearded man walked up to him. It was Geoff Tilden, the department head to whom Macgregor had reported during his employment at the California Air Pollution Research Institute.

"Got a minute?" asked Tilden. Peters nodded in reply. The two of them left the gravesite and walked along the winding road that led back to the parking lot.

"Ray was working on some pretty strange stuff when he died. Some of the staff think that he just went nuts. Some think that he might have been on to something. He was pretty excited toward the end, working long hours, chewing up computer time. Nobody's had a chance to go over his notes, not that he kept what you'd call reasonable documentation. But you've always been pretty good at figuring out what other people were after . . ." his voice trailed off.

"If you think that you've accidentally insulted me, you haven't. I know Ray was fond of telling people that I stole his work on the terpene mechanism. Steal from one and it's plagiarism. Steal from five and it's research. I do research."

"Well, okay," said Tilden, uncomfortably. "Whatever it is that you do, I know you're good at it. And I thought that maybe you could look over Ray's notes and papers and get an inkling of what he was working on. Maybe it was just crazy bullshit, but I'd hate to think that he nearly had something and just died too soon."

"You're not worried that I'll steal it, whatever it was?"

"Hell, what can you steal from a dead man?"

When he got out to his car, his headache had subsided a bit, but his desire for work had ebbed as well. Forget it, he told himself. It's been a bum day. Chuck it and go enjoy yourself, you have some slack due you.

He got into his car and drove north toward the hills and the allure of Shreiber Manse. Blot it all out, he thought. Everybody dies someday, but you don't have to go just right now.

The sky was cloudless blue with only a hint of haze. He looked at it with professional detachment. What little haze there was should burn off soon. Normally, there would be a lot more brown to it, in layers up through the inversion. Now it looked like the aftermath of a storm, scrubbed and fresh.

A hint of a scowl crossed his face. Now there was something odd. What was it? It looked like a bit of a ripple, a twinge of color just about where the base of the inversion should be. It seemed to move slightly, but he couldn't be sure that it wasn't an illusion, like the way electric power lines seem to move if you stare at them too long.

He couldn't take his eyes from the road for long. After a few minutes the illusion passed, fading into the background of peripheral perception. To hell with it, he thought. I officially declare this to be a hooky day. I am going to eat, and get drunk. I am going to party with friends. I am going to try to get laid.

It's not like this stuff is very important.

```
EXECUTION TRACE:   SMOGMOD IV
        LAGRANGIAN PUFF SUBMODEL
LOCATION:    40689.48, 1541.43 UTM COORDINATES
CELL (26.23,21.15)
            X        Y
TIME:   12:57:54
AVERAGE CONCENTRATIONS (PPM)
O₃              2240703
NO              * * * * * * * *
NO₂             * * * * * * * *
OLEFIN          * * * * * * * *
PARAFFIN        0.08
ETHENE          * * * * * * * *
AROMATIC        0.006
CO              0.54
H₂O₂            56100.92
HNO₂            0.0001
HNO₃            0.14
RADICAL CONCENTRATIONS NOT FILED
```

Wednesday Afternoon: Abrams

Abrams loved flying, especially in a blimp. It seemed
to him to be closer to dream-flying than any heavier-
than-air craft, even a glider, could ever be. One just
caught hold of a good air mass, switched off the
engines, and drifted with the wind.

The SCAQMD blimp was in many ways a perfect
device for monitoring air pollution. Up above the
confusion of freeways and other sources of pollutants that made surface monitoring a headache, one
could obtain nice, smooth averages of all the atmospheric junk. And you could play tag with a particular
parcel of air, watching as the concentrations increased, watching as the photochemical reactions
progressed, estimating with some degree of precision
just how long the parcel would stay within the Los
Angeles basin.

At the moment, Abrams was carefully watching
two devices, a Flame Ionization Detector (FID)
which gave readings for hydrocarbons, and a "NO_x
Box," a chemiluminescence detector, with a catalyst,
for the detection of oxides of nitrogen. Hydrocarbons and NO_x suitably cooked, yielded photochemical ozone, which had been low for the entire flight so
far. Abrams wanted to see if one or the other precursors were lacking.

"Total hydrocarbons have been running at a constant two parts per million," he said into the tape
recorder. "Not appreciably above background. I've
just taken a sample for chromatographic speciation,
but my guess is that total nonmethane hydrocarbons
are not above two-tenths of a ppm. Nitrogen oxides
are likewise very lean, near detection limits, no more
than ten parts per billion. I don't know what's happening to the emissions from down below, but they
certainly aren't *here*.

"I'm going to raise ship a bit, to see what's up in

the inversion." He notified the Air Traffic Control of his intent.

The sun was on its afternoon descent as he trickled some water out of the ballast tanks and went to negative buoyancy. The blimp began a slow rise. He kept an eye on the air-temperature gauge, awaiting the telltale increase that would inform him that he was penetrating the thermal inversion. When he reached the inversion, however, he needed no measurements to inform him of the fact.

"Whew!" he said. "I've just hit something or other; the temperature must have climbed a good ten degrees. My temperature gauge is still moving. And I'd swear that I could smell gasoline. Gasoline and auto exhaust. Wait a moment." He leaned over to an instrument gauge.

"The THC meter just pinned. Peak scale is twenty ppm, so we have one hell of a lot of hydrocarbons up here. The NO_x meter is still playing dead though, oops, spoke too soon. THC just dropped to background and the NO_x box just went bananas. This can't be right, there must be some malfunction, maybe the sudden heat did it. Oh, I've got a visual on something, back in a minute."

He scrabbled over to a viewport that faced west. There was something odd about the sky in the direction of the sunlight. He shaded his eyes to try to make it out. No, there were too many secondary reflections from the window. Although it was against protocol, he slipped the latches from the window and pulled the glass inside. That was better. There was some sort of ripple in the slight haze layer that he had penetrated. And a few little lumps, eddy currents maybe, moving toward him. . . .

The shock hit him like a blow to the chest. He coughed, tried to inhale and suddenly his lungs were on fire, sharp spikes in his sinuses, eyes misted over with red. He stumbled in his crouched position and the windowpane splintered beneath him.

His last thought before he died was of hellfire and damnation. They couldn't be any worse than this.

Wednesday Afternoon: The Children

At one of the corners of the grounds of Shreiber Manse, behind the tennis court and next to the gazebo, stood a modest cottage, originally intended for a groundskeeper. Shreiber employed a professional landscaping-and-gardening concern (which required no housing space) and he allowed three or four amateurs, including himself, latitude for puttering about. This puttering sometimes incurred the displeasure of the regular gardening staff. The incident of the tree grafts was still occasionally unfurled in moments of heat.

The cottage had become something of a hideaway for friends of the family and worthy persons in need. Currently it was inhabited by Marty Williams and her three children, on the run from a sometimes violent ex-husband and (maybe) the law. Shreiber did not ask about the latter possibility except to ascertain that there were no federal or California state warrants outstanding. No one ever mentioned South Dakota, and Shreiber expressly did not inquire. Peters had met Marty only briefly on his most recent visit, months before, just after she had moved in.

Next to the gazebo stood what perhaps might be called a jungle gym, but was generally referred to as "The Contraption." It looked like something that Dick Seaton might use to repel alien invaders. It had begun as one of Larry's experiments in psychic phenomena; one could still just barely make out the original pyramid form. But Larry, John, and Arthur had got to tinkering, trying for something other than an essentially negative result. They had succeeded to the extent that The Contraption was sufficient to startle an unprepared visitor.

Shreiber had merely commented that aesthetics were still more powerful than psi.

When Peters reached The Contraption it was swarming with kids, if seven can constitute a swarm. In addition to Anthony, Colby, and Trina, Marty's kids, Peters noted Helen and James from the nearest neighbors, Ben's niece Darlene, and Aya, Shreiber's eleven-year-old daughter from his first marriage.

Marty greeted him with a hug. "Hello, Walt," she said. "How is life up in fogland?"

"Cold and damp as ever," he said. "How are you? Life at the Manse seems to agree with you."

She opened her mouth to reply but was cut short by his startled laugh. Aya had detached herself from The Contraption and reattached herself to Peters's back.

"Hey!" he said, staggering a bit from the impact. "You've grown some more."

"Some more what?" she said, wrinkling her nose at her own joke.

"Some more pounds," he said. "Or maybe kilos. Any more and you may kilo me."

"Foo," she said. "I caught you fair and square. I don't let you go until you show me what you brought me."

"Materialist," he accused, reaching into his pocket.

"Romantic," she replied, hopping down.

By this time the rest of the children had dismounted The Contraption and had gathered around. Peters pulled some paper scissors from his pocket and tore a page from his notebook. As he folded and cut the paper, he repeated a bit of stage patter that he'd once heard from a magic show. The wonders of the East were invoked. He gave a paper bird to Aya.

The majesty of the Orient was emphasized. He presented three different kinds of paper flowers to Colby, Trina, and Anthony. Helen and John both received paper boxes, and he gave Darlene a paper frog while he finished with a poem in praise of gunpowder and opium. Marty grinned at him.

"Okay, now," he said. "Those are cute and nifty, but being able to make them is even cuter and niftier. So after you've gotten sick of having a damn fool cheap paper gift, then try taking them apart to see if you can remake them. Anybody who manages it can teach everybody else. If there's any you can't figure out, I'll teach you the day after tomorrow. Now I want one quick climb through The Contraption, and then I want to talk to Marty for a while, okay?"

The children agreed and then proceeded to show him the most difficult way through the maze of pipes and fittings. His undershirt was soaked when he finished. Marty had brought a couple of lawn chairs and a beer from the cottage. He accepted it greedily.

"Whew. Many thanks," he said. "That's quite a workout. Where were we?"

"I was about to tell you the good news," she said. "Monica pulled a few strings and we have an agent. The kids have already made a couple of commercials."

"Well hot damn," he said. "Good for all of you. That didn't really take much string-pulling, I'll bet. They're natural charmers, much like their mother."

She beamed at his flattery. "Thank you," she said. "The agency was impressed. I think that we looked just different enough to be intriguing, something besides the usual Hollywood flash. Monica says . . ."

A childish wail cut her off. Helen had missed a handhold and had bashed her ear on a pipe. "I didn't do it!" yelled John, as everyone gathered around Helen where she sat crying in the dirt.

"Right," Peters said to John. Then he settled

down beside Helen. "Here hon, let's see the damage." He cupped her jaw with his hand and turned her head so that he could see her ear.

"It's a bit red already," he told her. "So you may get a bruise. There's no permanent damage, but I'll bet it hurts, huh?" She nodded. Her cheeks were wet.

He caught her gaze and looked at her intently. He smiled. "Some of that pain is still real, but most of it is just memory, remembering how it hurt just a minute ago. So the best way to get rid of it is to give your ear something else to remember. In Sri Lanka they use feathers to banish the memory of pain, each stroke of the feather sends the pain a little farther away." He began to lightly stroke the scalp around her ear. "I don't have a feather with me, but if you'll pretend my hand is a feather we might be able to do the trick." He circled slowly around the redness, his touch becoming softer as he spoke. Finally he leaned over and blew in her ear. She tried to maintain her woeful expression, but it was clear that a giggle lurked just beneath the tear-stained surface. He grinned at her.

"We'll leave the rest for the Sri Lanka feathers." He reached into his pocket and pulled out one last origami flower.

"Just in case the bruise is unsightly and so's not to spoil your chances of landing a husband tomorrow, we'll pin this in your hair so it covers the offending area. It'll also serve as a cushion for the next time you beat up a cast-iron pipe with your ear." He stood up. "Up we go," he said, taking her hands and lifting her to her feet. "Do you think that you could get me another beer? Working feather magic with no feathers is thirsty work."

"I'll get it!" called John, racing off toward the cottage.

"No, he asked me!" Helen yelled and took off after him.

"You are about to be inundated with beer," said Marty, as the screen door to the cottage slammed twice.

He shrugged. "Better than uranium poisoning."

She raised one eyebrow. He explained, "Old engineering school joke. One treatment for uranium poisoning is beer, because heavy metals are excreted through the kidneys. Gallons of beer a day, in fact. So we used to rhapsodize about the joys of uranium, and contemplate the U-235 and beer cocktail, the nuclear boilermaker, the Budweiser meltdown."

When the two bottles arrived, he thanked the couriers and handed a beer to Marty. She took a long swallow. Then she said, "Have you had much experience with kids? You seem good with them."

He half-smiled. "To the best of my knowledge and recollection, I am childless." He leaned back in the lawn chair and closed his eyes.

"I know my limitations," he said. "Children are easily entertained. It's easy to be Uncle Walt with his snappy patter and shuck-and-jive. I can be anybody's perfect buddy for a day, the ideal father figure for a couple of hours, twice a month. But raising a kid? My own kid? That's a twenty-year project and a nine hundred percent commitment. I'm just a goddamn dilettante."

"You'd still make a better father than ninety percent of the men with kids. Not to mention my own ex."

"Only ninetieth percentile?" he said in a self-mocking tone. "Hell that lets me out. I don't do anything unless I can be ninety-ninth percentile."

They were both silent for a while, watching the kids clamber on The Contraption. Then she said, "You're right about it being a nine-hundred percent commitment, though. There isn't a thing I do that isn't affected by the children. I can't imagine life without them."

"I cheated a little bit there, I think," he said. "The nine hundred percent gets divided up fifty percent for the father and eight hundred and fifty for the mother. Another reason for not having kids. I've never found a woman that I'd be willing to take advantage of so thoroughly."

"It is the woman's choice, isn't it?"

"Yes," he admitted. "I've always believed that the human race was a selective breeding experiment carried out by women with men as domesticated animals sort of hauled along for the ride."

"So we get back to the original question," she said. "Why hasn't anyone hauled you along?"

"Too much shuck-and-jive?" he suggested.

She gave him a steely smile. "Maybe you're too proud to accept the position of domesticated animal."

The Minister

"And we *are* the modern Babylon! It lives around us. We see it every day. Yet all this too shall fall, as did Babylon, as did Persia, as did Rome. The good citizens of Pompeii could smell the brimstone in the air, but they did not heed its warning. Yet the Beast lives, and the stench of his breath should strike to the soul of any man.

"Now the Book of Revelations warns us of this Beast, and the prophet that is unto him. 'And the Beast was taken, and with him the false prophet that wrought miracles before him, with which he deceived them that had received the mark of the Beast, and them that had worshipped his image. These both were cast alive into a lake of fire burning with brimstone.'

"And just step outside and take a whiff! Can't you

smell the stench of hell? They worship the graven image of the factory and the oil refinery and the automobile, and the very air becomes thick with the fumes of it. How long must we walk the edge of the volcano before we realize that . . . ?''

Pastor Jackson put down his pen and sighed. Yes, a fine sermon if only the weather would cooperate. But hellfire and the whiff of brimstone won't go very far with days as beautiful as they have been. And the forecasters were way out in left field. No, he'd be better off ranting about the worship of Mammon, or drug addiction, or jungle music.

He got up and walked to the window. As it happened, he sometimes liked the sunsets that went along with the heavy smog days. He knew that they were probably the work of the devil, but he supposed that a fallen angel might occasionally let something innocuous slip by. He chided himself on that little bit of levity and turned back toward his desk. Too bad this day was going to have such a blah sunset. . . .

Something caught the corner of his eye as he turned and he turned back toward the window. What was that? A balloon? No, a blimp. Not very far away either, and descending. Funny, there was no landing field nearby.

The blimp hit a power line and the pastor gasped. It had crashed! Good Lord! The minister opened the window for a better view, then he went to the phone to call the emergency number.

For a brief moment, he thought he caught the smell of brimstone.

But he shrugged it off.

Wednesday Evening

Whap!

Peters winced as he watched Monica fly through the air and land noisily on her side. He knew that when properly done, *ukemi*, the art of taking a fall, allowed such a maneuver to be completed without damage. But he had once practiced aikido for six months and a badly separated shoulder had been his worst and final injury. Watching Monica brought back memories that he'd rather leave in a drawer with his now unused judo *gi*.

Colby sat next to Walter. "Mom says I can start learning this stuff next month, after my birthday. That'll be choice."

Peters shrugged. He wondered how Colby would take to the bruises and the general feeling of awkwardness that was the lot of all beginning students. Well, he'd find out. And he'd either get discouraged or he'd get better.

The class ended with formal bows from the instructors and students. Monica introduced Peters to some of her fellow students.

"Thanks for coming to pick me up, Walter," she said. "This is Mark and this is Koichi. They're my favorite *judoka*, at least when they're within earshot. Guys, meet Walter Peters, smog scientist extraordinaire."

The four exchanged a few more words, then suddenly Koichi called out, "Hiro! Stop that!"

Koichi's son, Hirotomi, and Colby were the object of attention. It turned out that Colby had been trying to show Hiro some trick that he had learned for getting out of a behind-the-back wrist lock. But Hiro was a judo student and had held Colby's wrist with a twist that made escape impossible. So Colby, too embarrassed to cry uncle, had thrashed around until Hiro had released him for fear of hurting him. A scuffle threatened, but Koichi and Monica stopped it quickly.

"Colby," said Monica sweetly. "How would you like to start getting knocked on your ass ahead of schedule?"

"But he . . ." Colby began and then quickly stopped when Monica took a step toward him.

Hiro was very quiet. Koichi said something in Japanese and Hiro turned and hurried from the room.

"Go after him and apologize," Monica told Colby. "Or I'll tell your mother."

When both boys had left, Monica asked Koichi, "What did you say to him?"

"Pretty much the same as you; I threatened to tell his mother."

"Usually it's the mother threatening to tell the father," Monica said.

"Not in our house. My wife is a third-degree black belt."

It was game night in Shreiber Manse. Peters finished dinner, took a shower, and then began a slow tour through the Manse in search of interesting company.

The library was devoted to chess, as was always the case on game night. After kibitzing for a few minutes, Peters realized that the matches were far above his level and moved on.

The room that held the nitrous tank had been dubbed the "Ruckus Room." Two games proceeded here: Fairy Scrabble and Dungeons and Dragons. Fairy Scrabble differed from ordinary Scrabble in that only invented words were allowed, with definitions to be supplied upon demand. Words whose definitions included malapropisms, spoonerisms, or puns counted double.

The most notable feature of the D & D game was its dungeonmaster, Jim Vibber, a man with a wicked sense of humor. The gameplayers had just passed through the magic pyramid (which sharpened all of their swords and kept their food fresh) when they were set upon by a horde of Jewish grannies, intent upon immobilizing the heroes by guilt and overfeeding. The battle was horrendous.

Peters found Monica at the poker game, where she was winning her third straight pot.

"The secret is a clear head, a calm body, and cheating," she explained. "Hi, Walter," she said to Peters. "Want to join the game?"

"I thought I'd see what Doug is up to," he said.

She pointed. "Auction Monopoly is in the west corner bedroom, first floor."

It was Doug Shreiber's theory that games should be classified into poor, good, and great. Bridge was an example of a poor game and he banned it from the Manse. "All you learn from bridge is how to play bridge," he explained. "A pure waste of time."

Great games on the other hand expanded the mind and taught you something fundamental about life and your fellow gamesmen. The only certain examples of great games that he had found so far were chess, *go*, and poker. Chess was complexity itself, whereas *go* was profound. Both were indicators of precision of intellect. Poker was a nearly ideal metaphor for life in the modern society, the importance of chance, and the need to bluff and lie.

Auction Monopoly was the most recent candidate for the great game pantheon. Unlike regular Monopoly, auction Monopoly required all players to bid for property when anyone landed on it. The game therefore showed all of the characteristics of a monetary economy: inflation, deflation, overextended investments, and monetary collapse. Shreiber was still tinkering with the rules, however, which he maintained only increased the realism. He was wondering how to institute a Federal Reserve Board, and whether the members should be susceptible to bribery or merely to political influence.

"I hereby call a bank holiday," he said. "Everyone stretch, smoke 'em if you got 'em. Back here in fifteen minutes." He looked at Peters. "You look a little more together than you did this afternoon. Did the nap help?" Peters had passed out on the couch earlier in the day. He hadn't known that he was that tired.

"Yeah. I feel much better. This place is great for forgetting about the real world." Shreiber bowed, taking the other's words as a compliment, which they were.

"It's not like you to get this wrapped up in the job," said Shreiber. "Just what's causing all the big fuss?"

"Well, when I came down, I thought that it was just a modeling problem. Somebody input a wrong rate constant, somebody thinks that cars put out pure ethylene, something like that, only probably more subtle. But it turns out to be a bona-fide mystery. It's not just our model that's not predicting the smog behavior of the past few days. It's everything. Statistical regression models agree with the photochemical dispersion models, which agree with the expert judgment of local meteorologists and air-pollution control personnel. Everything that we know says that it should be smoggy, and it's not."

"So that's bad?"

"You've worked with statistical models. When a positive correlation vanishes overnight, you get worried. Something new has been added. Look, it turns out that the single greatest determinant of smog intensity is air temperature aloft. That's because it links to so many of the underlying processes. High temperatures cause greater hydrocarbon emissions from evaporation, vegetation emits more hydrocarbons and soaks up less oxidants, the photochemistry works faster and the thermal inversion becomes more intense. The temperature aloft today is high, not a record, but pretty high. But the air was clean this morning. It's enough to give you the willies.''

He shrugged and scratched his beard. "Oh well, we shouldn't complain. Maybe nature has changed a few laws for our benefit. That would be nice. Say, did I ever tell you about smog and the price of soybeans?''

Shreiber shook his head so Peters continued. "It goes like this: As I said, the greatest correlation to smog intensity is with temperature aloft, which determines atmospheric stability. Temperature aloft is a result of large scale, synoptic air flows into the area generally from the southwest, from over the ocean. So ocean temperature and the placement of ocean currents has a major influence.''

"Now it turns out that a similar condition exists off the coast of Peru, where they occasionally get a type of storm system that they call El Niño. Then the cold water currents off the South American coast wander a bit, and instead of warm stable air, they get cold, moist, unstable air that causes major storms along the Peruvian coast.

"El Niño also wipes out the anchovy schools because the nutrient upwelling from the ocean bottom temporarily ceases when the currents shift.

"As a former commodities speculator, you may be aware that the principal use of anchovy is for high-protein animal feed, where it competes with soybeans. So some soybean traders watch for El Niño, because that means more pressure on the soybean market.

"So if anyone ever asks you what smog has to do with the price of soybeans, you send them to me.''

The Monster

It did not know sleep, but its sleep was ending. It did not know awareness, but awareness drifted into its world; its dark spaces became light. It did not know action, but it was becoming active. Parameters changed, shifted. Inputs twitched. Reactants blended. Fantasies merged. Energy was released. Power.

Inside it was a seed, a kernel of rage. All else was a cloak that gave it form, connections, abilities. But its essence was rage.

All its dreams were now the same dream, a patchwork of red. A glowering.

It stirred. It dreamed of its own incandescent core. It dreamed the sun.

Thursday Morning

The next day was ugly. The early morning fog did not burn off; the murk intensified, its hue darkening to shades of umber, yellow, and brown. A dry and acrid stench pressed down upon all who stepped outside. Indoors, nauseous little tendrils of the stuff would become noticeable from time to time, reminding everyone of the filth outside and making tempers short.

"Stage-two alert has already been called," Mei Lin informed him when he walked through the door. "Word has it that stage three is only an hour or two away. There hasn't been a stage three since they made up the classifications, although I understand that there were some days in the fifties that probably would have qualified."

"Probably," Peters told her. "We'll never know for sure. Calibration standards are different now.

Back then they measured total oxidant rather than ozone and wet chemical methods are fussy. For that matter some investigators were still using rubber crack depth as late as the early sixties. Now there's a reproducible methodology for you.''

"So what gives? Was Big Daddy smog just saving it up for a real doozy?"

"I wish to hell I knew."

The telephone complaint lines were swamped. People complained of burning eyes, shortness of breath, sudden coughing spasms. Acute asthmatics were forced to their beds. Some of the telephone respondents were belligerent; some threatened mayhem or murder. All were told to stay indoors, avoid exertion, and try not to use their automobiles.

The last prescription was generally ignored. This was southern California, after all.

The SCAQMD offices took on the characteristics of a crisis center. A large chalkboard was commandeered to show the status of the episode. Ozone monitors in Pomona, Fontana, and Redlands were showing spikes that went clear offscale. San Fernando Valley observers reported that the San Fernando convergence zone, a minifrontal system in the wake of the Santa Monica mountains, had become clearly visible, a reddish brown column of air.

Wade Smith, manager of the upper-air monitoring group, came in late in the afternoon. He had a stricken look about him.

"Abrams is dead," he said dully. All activity ceased and the researchers crowded around.

"What happened?" asked Mei Lin.

He shook his head. "The blimp came down in Chino, sometime last evening. It got smashed up a bit. A couple of us went down; they were just taking his body away when we got there. Maybe he died in the crash, but . . ."

"What is it?"

"His hair. His skin. They were white. His hair looked like a bad bleach job, like someone forgot to dilute the peroxide. And the look on his face . . ." He closed his eyes.

Peters walked over to the window. The sun would begin to set soon. Probably be one glorious sunset, smoggy days were known for it. A sudden chill ran down his spine.

"Too bad there's no such thing as a stage four alert," he said.

Williams

"Well, Mr. Williams, this has been a middling difficult case; here's my bill along with your wife's current address.

"It was relatively easy tracing your children, through the commercials you showed me, to the talent agency that handles them. However, the agency was reticent about giving out any additional information, as one might expect. I did contrive to be left alone in the office for a few moments, however, and I managed to get a post office box number.

"Most of the bill is taken up in the costs of staking out the postal box—that may be a crime, so please don't tell anyone about it. Fortunately, the lines in this post office are as long as they are anywhere, and most of the boxes are visible from the main area. So we had several men go through the lines in succession, watching the pertinent P.O. box.

"The stakeout only lasted for a day and a half, but it took five men. The box was opened by a tall brunette whom we have identified as Monica Shreiber, originally Monica Clawson, a minor movie actress. Your wife Marty is staying at the Shreiber estate. Mr. Shreiber is quite wealthy and on good terms with the police so I advise discretion in your attempts at reconciliation with your estranged wife.

"Mrs. Shreiber used to be a client of the Lewis Talent Agency, the firm handling your children. It pays to have influential friends, don't you agree?"

Shreiber Manse sat far back in one of the canyons in Beverly Glen. It was elevated and isolated, so that the smog from Los Angeles was only a muted pressure. Even on this night, in the midst of the worst smog episode in memory (which is to say the worst episode ever) the air seemed reasonable going down the throat. But Peters's eyes still burned slightly from the drive back, as he staggered in through the door.

"You look like hell," said Monica.

"I've been there," he told her.

She poured him a stiff drink and he wandered into the Ruckus Room. A general confab was in session; some of the people seemed to be discussing science fiction.

"I finally managed to sell a story to *High Tech, The Magazine of Future Fiction*," some woman was saying. Peters vaguely remembered having met her before. Her name was Dorothy something or other. "It's called 'Moment of Inertia' and it's a locked-room mystery. The detection hinges on the fact that the angular momentum of a hollow object is greater than that of a solid one, provided both have the same mass. I also manage to introduce the concept of a love tetrahedron which involves four people, two of whom have to be bisexual . . ."

Ben and Johnny, computer programmers whom Peters knew to be originally from New York, were over in a corner discussing Max Ernst and Milo Duke, and reading fanzines, mostly ones produced by science fiction fans, but including some punk and new wave music publications. They were mimeographed and generally hideous to behold, but once in a while someone would read a section aloud and the chosen passage would be hilarious—sometimes intentionally so.

"Hey, Doug," said Larry-who-drew-comic-books. "Didn't you once hang out with a lot of science fiction fans?"

"Yeah," said Shreiber. "I used to call them sci-fi buffs, though. They really hate that, it doesn't sound like you take it seriously, which they usually do, and I didn't."

"Is that why you quit, then? They took it too seriously?"

"I dunno, maybe. It began to all sound the same after a while. It became boring. But I think what really got to me was the snobbery. There were two big clubs in the area, the Bug-Eyed Monsters and Subsfa, the suburban science fiction association. I finally realized that the BEMs weren't interested in you unless you had a Ph.D. and Subsfa didn't notice you unless you had written a fantasy novel."

"But you *have* a Ph.D. and you've written a fantasy novel."

"Yeah, but none of them do, or have, so what do I need them for?"

Peters finished his drink and called out to Monica to please bring him another one quickly or he'd probably . . .

He didn't want to say the word *die.*

"Hey, Walter," sang out a redhead named Gloria, from the corner. "Smog's back. Are you happy?"

"No," was all he said, but the look on his face made someone ask, "Are you all right?"

"No," he said again, stupidly hoping that they would all shut up and leave him alone.

"What's wrong, Walter?" asked Monica as she handed him a fresh drink. He took a gulp.

"Somebody died, that's all," he said.

"Who died?" a girl asked.

"How did it happen?" asked someone else.

"You don't know him. He was a smog researcher, a pilot."

"Hey, I heard something about that on the radio. It was a blimp that crashed. A research balloon. It said that he died in the crash."

"Well, he didn't," said Peters in a sneering voice. "He was bleached to death." Nobody snickered. He got up and left the room. Maybe a swim would help.

He went out to the pool and stripped off his clothes. There were no lights in the pool area and the Manse was loose in its dress code in any event. He dove in. The shock of the cool water wiped away the fog of the drinks. Damn it, he thought. Now I'll have to start over.

Monica was waiting for him when he climbed out. She had brought a robe. "Take this," she said. "On clear nights it gets pretty cold up here in the hills."

The night was clear and it was growing cold. He put on the robe and sat down on a poolside lounging chair. Monica sat on the near end of the diving board. He could see her face in the dim light that made it from the house.

"Is it true?" she asked. "What you said about that man's dying? Is that why you're so upset?"

"I'm upset because I don't know what's happening." He shook his head. "In research it's common to be baffled and confused. That goes with the territory. But you always have the feeling that there are rules to things, if only you can figure them out. It's not witchcraft. It's just a pattern too complicated to figure out easily. But you know the general outlines of the problem and the general outlines of the solution.

"But what's been happening lately is impossible. There's no pattern to it except that it defies all the rules. And the pilot's death, well that just caps it.

"Dammit, nobody dies of smog! Blizzards kill people. Cars kill people, cigarettes kill people, knives and guns and bathtubs kill people, but smog is not lethal. It's ugly and annoying and it burns your eyes and gives you a headache. If you have asthma it might set off an attack, if you have allergies it might make them worse. Maybe an emphysemic with a bad heart will die during a smog alert, but that puts smog in there with all the other stresses of modern life. You can learn to live with it, if you have to; most people do.

"But Abrams's death scares me. It scares me way down in my gut where I can't reason with it. How can I? Reason tells me that it can't happen. His hair was bleached. How much oxidant does that take? How much ozone and peroxide? A hundred times more than anybody's ever seen? A thousand times? That's crazy. I keep telling myself that it's a mistake, Wade couldn't have seen what he saw, Abrams just died in the crash, and there's some logical reason why we're in the midst of a smog episode that came up out of nowhere and that nobody can explain. I tell myself all that and I can't get myself to believe it. I just get scared."

"I should think you'd be excited. A new phenomenon. Unraveling the mysteries of the universe. All that stuff."

"I know. I feel like a fake. The guy's real good at the easy ones, but let him get a whiff of big-league pitching and he chokes. I hate myself for it.

"But I can't help it. I keeping thinking that I'm like a geologist standing on the side of Mount St. Helens just before she blows."

Interlude

From the taped notes of Douglas Albert, M.D. May 12, 198__. Case history of Henry C____, Marketing Executive

"Should I sit in the chair or lie on the couch? What? Oh yeah, I guess it could be taken that way, couldn't it. Yeah, to tell the truth I probably would feel a bit weird on the couch. I'll sit here.

"I'm not sure how to explain all of it. Why I'm here, I mean. I want to say something dramatic, like I've had a hex placed on me. It feels that way sometimes. I also sort of feel that I had it coming, too, but maybe that's a symptom.

"But hey, enough rambling, let's begin at the beginning, let's talk about it.

"I was divorced two, no three years ago, now. I ran pretty wild after the breakup. That's common enough. There's a lot of places in this city where good-looking chicks practically grow on trees. And money, charm, and good drugs go a long way, if you know what I mean. I figured, hell, my chance at a family was blown away, I owed it to myself and all my fellows who didn't have it so good to live out a few fantasies.

"Well, anyway, so I did a lot of cruising. It gets automatic after a while. And you get real good at spotting other people on the make. Hell, I've picked up girls at carwashes. You get to recognize the look. And if you don't mind striking out sometimes, you can get quite a few runs batted in.

"Huh? Yeah, I did. In college. Shortstop, because I had a long reach.

"Where was I? Oh yeah. Cruising.

"So I was cruising one night. Making the rounds of a few favorite spots. To tell the truth, I'm not sure which one it was. No wait, now I remember. The Viceroy. It's not quite a pickup joint. Too cool maybe. But it happens often enough. It's a good scene.

"I was halfway through my first drink when I noticed her. It was a shock, a surprise. It was like being in a room that you thought was empty and having someone brush your elbow. I still don't know how I overlooked her when I came in. She was beautiful, but more than that, she was striking. Just sitting there she exuded a sort of grace, without moving, she reminded me of a cat. A body like . . . Whew. Dark hair with a streak in it, high cheekbones . . .

"And she was looking at me.

"I felt it in the pit of my stomach. And right between the eyes. She smiled at me and the next thing that I knew, I was sitting across from her.

"She asked me my name, and I told her. She said her name was Joella. Then she asked me a few more questions and I made with a bit of clever repartee and I was just about to ask her to go somewhere with me when she took my hand and stood up. I stood up with her and we headed for the door.

"I tried to be clever. 'How did you do that?' I asked her. 'Do what?' she asked me. 'Read my mind.' I said. 'I was just about to ask you if you wanted to leave.' 'Your place?' she said. 'Your place is closer.' 'Yeah,' I said. 'Like that. You read my mind.' She just smiled at me. 'It's easy,' she said. 'I'm a witch.'

"So we went back to my place. I made us a couple of drinks and then I laid out a few lines of coke. I offered some to her and all of a sudden I got the feeling that she was very amused. Like I'd just done something that was touching but maybe a bit gauche. She touched her finger to one of the lines and she tasted it. She had this little half smile on her the whole time. Then she told me, 'Tell you what,' she said. 'Let's play a little game. Let's go to bed, and the first time you get bored or tired or something, we'll do the coke.' While she was talking she had started to undress the both of us. I can't describe how she did it; all I can say is that I've never felt that good just getting undressed.

"It was . . . oh Christ! I can't even begin to . . . I could get explicit if you want, but it wouldn't get the idea across. Sometimes it felt as if my whole being was being pulled and compressed into a ball of energy. When we balled there were times when it felt like I was having a permanent orgasm and then I'd have a big one and we'd cool off for a little while and then she'd start me up again.

"We eventually got around to doing the coke; to tell the truth I'd forgotten about it. But we'd started talking and caressing in between bouts of going at it, and somewhere along the line she reached over and offered me some of my own coke. For some reason that seemed really funny, and we laughed so hard that we almost spilled the coke. Then we did the lines and then we made love again and then we talked for a while longer.

"I'm pretty sure I did most of the talking. She asked a lot of questions but it didn't feel like she was prying or anything; it was just the most natural thing in the world to answer. And I got to talking about life, and business, and even my childhood and my busted-up marriage. It's a good thing I don't know any defense secrets, because I would have spilled everything that night. I just couldn't shut up.

"Eventually I drifted off to sleep. I had a lot of strange dreams, I think, but I don't remember any of them. I woke up a few times during the night and there she was beside me, so beautiful and so peaceful, I was ready to marry her the next day. I remember thinking to myself that this was certainly a fish that I didn't want to throw back into the sea.

"When I woke up the next morning though, she wasn't there beside me. I heard a few noises from the next room and for a little while I thought that she'd gotten up to go to the bathroom or maybe fix breakfast. But all of a sudden I realized that she was leaving.

"I jumped out of bed and caught her as she was going out the door. 'Where are you going?' I asked her. 'Home,' she said. 'Where do you live?' I asked her. 'Give me your telephone number. I want to see you again.' She looked at me with the same sort of amusement as when I had offered her the coke.

" 'I don't want you to leave,' I told her. 'I love you.'

" 'Don't be a toad,' she told me. 'You don't even know my last name.'

"Then she opened the door and left me with my mouth still hanging open. The last thing that she said was, 'Don't worry. There are plenty of fish left in the sea.' Then she was gone.

"Now I've had chicks play games with me before. Usually I'd realize that she was playing games and I could say to myself, 'Fuck her, there *are* plenty of fish in the sea.' And even the really bad ones are usually gone in a day or two. A day at the beach, a little nightlife, lovesick blues are not that hard to lick.

"I thought.

"But this one busted me up good. I felt completely used, tricked, helpless. And I still wanted her so bad it like gave me cramps. I could barely force food down at mealtimes. I missed several days of work and when I went back everybody was really sympathetic; said I looked terrible and maybe I should take more time off. I got to feeling really sorry for myself.

"Finally I said, 'Enough is enough,' so I went out cruising again. But it wasn't the same. I couldn't get very interested. I found myself asking guys I met if they'd seen this chic with the dynamite body and the white streak in her hair. No one had seen her.

"And I was just plain awkward. I couldn't think of things to say. I'd been so clever; now I was just a gawping idiot. Even a gawper scores sometimes, but they weren't much fun. Especially the ones who seemed to do it out of pity. Then I started to not be able to get it up. I'd be with some girl and I'd start comparing her to Joella and it would be all over.

"So I don't know what to say. I'm not even sure what the problem is. Why can't I forget this one girl that I fucked once? Why am I so depressed all the time. What's wrong with me?

"Witch? Damn her eyes. She's a witch all right. She turned me into a toad."

PART TWO

L.A. WOMAN

Friday: Peters

He got up late the next morning and it took him a long time to get started. He had a hangover. He cursed himself as an idiot; he had never been able to handle liquor.

The drive to L.A. was nasty. All the other drivers seemed to be as irritable and belligerent as he felt. Well, how could it be otherwise? he asked himself. Just look at the sky.

The sky looked mean. The yellow and brown had visible swirls to it. In some places the color was so deep that it verged on black. It was hot, but he didn't dare roll down his window. The air was so astringent that it brought tears to the eyes and interfered with vision.

He turned on the radio.

. . . under a condition of smog emergency since ten o'clock this morning, when three monitoring stations reported ozone levels in excess of sixty parts per hundred million. Sensitive individuals are urged to stay indoors. Motorists have been asked to keep all driving to an absolute minimum. So don't drive unless you have to. Thousands are leaving the city for an early weekend; routes I-5, I-15, and 101 outbound have large traffic jams and the authorities have requested that people postpone . . .

He turned off the radio with a grimace.

The California Air Pollution Research Institute

was a private not-for-profit consulting organization that had once been affiliated with a nearby university. He pulled into the CAPRI parking lot a little before noon. Geoff Tilden came down to meet him at the front desk.

"Glad you could make it, Walter," said Geoff. "It may seem kind of strange, but the place is almost deserted. We don't do much in the way of monitoring work here, most of our people are mainly theoretical, so we've not been much use during this current mess. A lot of the guys are at home, like good little citizens, obeying the requests not to drive."

Peters shrugged. "I'm staying at a place that's fairly close to here. I didn't want to travel all the way to El Monte, so this seemed like a good day to look over Ray's notes. Besides, if he had any new ideas, we could probably use them. Regular theory seems to have jumped out the window."

"I'll take you to his office."

Macgregor's office was at the end of a long, seldom used corridor. "Most of the offices are used for dead storage," said Tilden. He winced. "I didn't mean that the way it sounded. Anyway, Ray took his office down here as a temporary measure when we were short of workspace. But later when I tried to move him, he refused. He said he liked the peace and quiet."

"That's strange," said Peters. "Ray didn't used to be like that. He spent a lot of time talking to people, picking their brains." He shrugged. "Well, people do change."

Tilden indicated a door. "Here's his office." The doorknob had been removed. Peters stared at the hole. "Somehow, Ray changed the lock on his door. We found out about it when we tried to get in. He wasn't supposed to do that. We had to remove the entire lock assembly. That's when we found him dead."

"How long had he been dead?"

"Only about a day. He didn't show up for a meet-ing, somebody came here to get him, found the door locked. When we tried to use a passkey, that didn't work, so we got maintenance to remove the lock. It was quite a surprise to the guy who first went in."

"I'll bet."

The office was cluttered with stacks of papers, reports, manuals, and other odds-and-ends all piled haphazardly on metal worktables and shelves. A computer terminal graced one of the walls. In the corner, underneath a table, sat a small refrigerator.

"What the hell is that?" asked Peters. On a table in another corner were several odd objects, including an antique retort and what seemed to be a skull, used as a candleholder.

"Yeah, we thought that was pretty weird. Looks a bit like something out of a horror-movie set, doesn't it? I never saw any of that stuff before. . . . My guess is that it's decoration. Like I said, Ray was getting pretty strange toward the end. I think that he was developing some affectations, like some people take to wearing opera capes with little stuffed dragons on their shoulders."

The air conditioning for the entire wing had been shut down to conserve power. It was hot outside, yet there was a chill dank feeling to the air in the office. Peters shivered slightly and Tilden noticed the tremor.

"You feel it too, eh?" said Tilden. "This room seems to run about five degrees colder than the rest of the building, we're not sure why. It seems even colder than that sometimes. Pretty Gothic, I'd say."

He tried a chuckle that was only slightly off the mark. "Anyway, here it all is, we haven't touched any of it, nobody has had the time. Stay here as long as you like. I'll notify the guards that you're here and that you're not to be disturbed."

Peters thanked him and Tilden left.

As he expected, Macgregor's notes were a mess. Peters set out to first try to arrange them into some sort of chronological order, a task made more difficult by the fact that Macgregor had used a private shorthand that was even more difficult to decipher than his cramped, angular handwriting. Eventually, he noticed that Macgregor's handwriting had become more and more jagged as time had passed, and this facilitated the ordering of it. It made the interpretation more difficult, however.

It was late in the afternoon before he had figured out enough of the shorthand to be able to make some sense out of some of the notes. One entry in particular caught his eye. It had been written about six months before, at just about the time when Macgregor had begun to deteriorate. It said: *If what J says can be believed, then it might be possible to formulate a model in such a way as to make it self-validating*.

From that point on, the notes made occasional cryptic references to SVMP, self-validating model project, was Peters's surmise. But the context of the notes made it impossible to figure out what it was supposed to do or how it was supposed to work. Most of what he could figure out seemed like ravings.

Shortly after five o'clock, he went down to the end of the hall for some water and to go to the restroom. He noticed that the whole building now sounded deserted; everyone had apparently packed it in early.

When he returned, there was someone in Macgregor's office.

It was a woman; his start of surprise at seeing her made her turn around from where she stood leaning over the table with the weird paraphernalia. A momentary look of surprise crossed her face and then she spoke.

"Hello," she said. "I thought everyone had left."

Her voice suited her appearance, rich and deep and dark. Her hair was long and black, almost Oriental in texture; it had a single white streak running down the left side. Her face and body were so striking that he was startled a second time. "What are you doing?" he blurted. "How did you get in here?"

She smiled. "The guard let me in."

"He's not supposed to do that."

" 'I have always depended upon the kindness of strangers.' " She said it flatly.

His surprise began to diminish. "Yeah, I'll bet. But what are you doing here?"

"I suspect that my aim is similar to yours. I am trying to discover what Ray Macgregor was doing before he died."

"Did you know Ray?"

"Somewhat. We were lovers for a time."

A thought occurred to him. "What's your name?"

"Joella," she replied.

"Are you the J that his notes sometimes refer to?"

"Perhaps. May I see the reference?"

He showed her. She said, "I think that this might refer to me. I do not understand any of this other though."

"Are you a scientist?" he asked.

"Not in the way that the term is properly used," she said. "I am more properly labeled a witch."

Uh-oh, he thought. A southern California loon. If Ray got mixed up with her that might explain why he went off the deep end.

She shook her head. "Please do not think of me in that way," she said. "I do not engage in conjuring tricks nor do I inflict mystical claptrap upon others. If the term witch offends you, think of me as a lay psychologist. That's only shady, not offensive."

She took a step forward. "Also please note that you have no desire to call the guard and have me removed. Raymond became insane in the days before he died. We need to find out if that insanity died with him or if it lives on in some manner.''

"What do you mean by that?"

"I wish that I knew." She walked back to the table and opened a leatherbound text that had been lying there. (Why had he not noticed that book before? It seemed quite old and its binding had a strange tooled design.)

"Raymond made some notations in the margins of this text," she said. "I cannot understand them. Some of the symbols are familiar, some are beyond me." She pointed to an equation.

He scowled. "Yes, I see what you mean. It looks like gibberish. The sort of thing that you see in a movie, produced by someone's just stringing together a lot of symbols from a math textbok, without knowing what they mean." He pointed to a mark. "That's a laplacean, and that over there might be a diffusivity tensor. I'll be damned if I know what that one is."

She smiled. "That is an alchemical symbol for aether," she said. "Between the two of us we may know more of this than we think."

He shook his head, frowning. "So Ray was trying some kind of nonsense blend of science and witchcraft? That's pretty hard to swallow."

"I agree. I can make no sense of it. I know of no precedent for it. I do not even know what I am looking for."

"Ah," he said. "I have an advantage on you there at least. I know what I'm looking for; I'm looking for a password. Most of his work was done on the computer terminal over there. But in order to gain access to his files, I need to know the password that he was using. Here, I'll show you."

He went over to the terminal and switched it on. It emitted a little *bleep* and the cursor mark appeared in the upper lefthand corner.

"Ray would have been using a computing network called EPANET for any environmental research. This terminal is connected directly to a small mainframe here in this building which is in turn connected by phone line to EPANET. Whenever his computing requirements exceeded what was available locally, the operating system would tap into a shared pool of spare capacity available from all users of the network."

He typed: LOGIN MACGREGOR

The machine responded:

```
MACGREGOR LOGGED IN 17:44:08
PASSWORD:  ⊗⊗⊗⊗⊗⊗⊗⊗⊗⊗⊗⊗
```

"Now I have to respond with the appropriate password. Let's try the project number that he was bootlegging all of this under." He typed in the numbers. The machine responded:

```
PASSWORD:  ⊗⊗⊗⊗⊗⊗⊗⊗⊗⊗⊗⊗
```

"See, it didn't buy it. Wrong password. Well, somebody once told me that six out of ten passwords ten characters or longer are 'Doonesbury.' So . . ." He typed again.

. . . and got

```
PASSWORD:  ⊗⊗⊗⊗⊗⊗⊗⊗⊗⊗⊗⊗
```

"Nope. That's not it. We could try 'Zonker' but I don't think so," he said. "On a hunch, how do you spell your name again?" She told him. "Let's see if Ray was a romantic." He typed J - O - E - L - L - A.

The machine replied:

```
MACGREGOR (1) ILLEGAL UFD/PROJECT CODE
Sorry, unable to log you in.
OK, LOGOUT
MACGREGOR (1) LOGGED OUT AT 17:45:43
TIME USED 0:00    0:01    0:00
```

"Well, so he wasn't romantic," he said. "We could keep this up forever, but I don't think we'll get anywhere until . . ."

She yelled, "Look out!" and pushed him aside with a strength that briefly surprised him. Then all his thoughts were cut short as the CRT screen imploded, followed by the sound of smashing plastic as the office window sagged and exploded inward.

Many years previous, when he was a young boy playing with his first Gilbert chemistry set, he had followed the directions for the making of ammonia. Only instead of boiling the reagents on a spoon and letting it waft into his nostrils, he had collected the gas in a test tube. Unsure of the yield, he had then taken a deep breath from the mouth of the tube. The sudden shock had literally knocked the breath out of him.

This was similar, but much worse. After the first explosive cough, his throat closed, refusing to accept any more of what was given to it. He stumbled, fell, and rolled into a ball, trying to protect his bare skin from the feeling of being scalded. Through closed eyes, images came to him in shades of brown and red.

Dimly, he heard a voice, rasping but loud:

"Nach dem Namen von Bach und Beethoven,
Nach Namen von Einstein und Shrödinger,
Nach Max Planck, Helmholtz, und Haagen-Smit
Packe dich!
Alles unharmonisch und unordentlich Formen
und Einflusse auf einmal gehen Sie aus!"

The words repeated. The pain that surrounded him diminished. Slowly, the world returned to normal. After what seemed forever, he risked drawing a breath. His throat was scratchy and it hurt to breathe. He couldn't tell how bad the air was, his perceptions had been overwhelmed. Everything stank of ozone and burnt linen.

"Peroxy acetyl nitrate," he said to himself, as if the naming of it was an incantation. "PAN and O_3, that 'excited state of life-giving oxygen.' " He wondered if he was in shock.

"Are you all right?" she said, kneeling beside him.

"Are you?" he asked in reply. "How did you manage to say anything while *that* was going on? I couldn't even breathe."

"I felt it coming and took a deep breath before the window broke," she told him. "Besides, its principal attack was at you."

"Why? What was it?"

"A smog demon."

He blinked and shook his head. "Run that one by me again?"

"You were attacked by a smog demon. One of the smaller incarnations of the larger entity that now threatens Los Angeles. I believe that it attacked you because you attempted to penetrate its nature without protection."

He tried getting up and succeeded on the second attempt, with her help. He steadied himself. He leaned against a bookshelf for support.

"Am I completely scrambled? Are you saying that that thing hit here because I just tried to log onto Ray's computer files?"

"I believe that to be a reasonable theory; a possible interpretation of events," she said.

He sagged against the bookshelf, then straightened. He looked at the wreckage of the office. "Let's get out of here," he said.

Peters's car crouched alone in the parking lot.

"No," Joella said. "My car is across the street. We use my car."

He looked up into the brown and ugly sky. At the edges of vision he saw movements that were not quite movement, like hallucinatory ripples in a still pond. He felt naked, exposed.

She nodded. "Yes, it's still up there. We must move quickly."

They reached her car, a small pale blue Audi. "Close the sunroof," she ordered as they got in. She accelerated so fast that he nearly broke the handle that cranked the roof.

"Hey!" he exclaimed.

"Seat belt." She smiled at him, then she took a sharp right turn with a four-wheel drift at nearly sixty. He managed to fasten the seat belt just as she hit the brakes. They slowed with a squeal of tires and took the last two blocks to the freeway entrance five miles below the speed limit.

"Keep low and keep moving," Peters muttered. "They shoot at the shadows."

She glanced at him sideways. "Exactly. The creature cannot see us. His senses are coarse. We need camouflage, motion, and unpredictability."

She accelerated and merged with the traffic flow.

Joella slid the Audi in and out of the traffic patterns, first into the fast lane, overtaking a gray BMW, playing tag with it as both vehicles teased each other toward ninety. Then suddenly, she stroked the brakes, and placidly moved over a lane, settling in between two trucks.

"This is not working," she said. "The presence is too strong here. If the freeway jams, we'll be exposed. We may have to run for it, leave the car . . ."

Peters thought to himself. Do I believe all this? Can smog really be alive, with a brown cloud for a body, a simulation model for a soul?

Suppose you want clean air for a few days? Simple, crank up the antidiffusion terms in the transport algorithm and make it chemical species specific.

Separate your hydrocarbons from the nitrogen oxides. Let the animal build up its reserves, like fat cells in a newborn. Like baby fat.

Or how about a killer whirlwind? How about a Lagrangian puff submodel? A sentient whirlwind would be a Lagrangian creature. A lesser demon.

The image of the freeways flashed at him, the emissions network that was the life's blood of a smog creature. Of course his presence would be strong here. This is the wellspring of his power. This is where his perceptions are most acute.

"The hills," he blurted. "Uneven terrain and winding roads. Use surface streets to get there."

Joella slashed across three lanes of traffic to reach the exit. Horns blared, then suddenly a wall of brakelights appeared just down the freeway, past the exit ramp. "Looks like we just made it," Peters said.

"The middle button is traffic," she said, indicating the radio.

They stayed on Pico for only a few seconds, then Joella hauled left on Carmelina and then quickly right on Tennessee. Then another left, and Peters began to feel like he was on a downhill slalom.

"KDIG, all news, weather and traffic. Today, of course, they're all just about the same thing. We have a special report on the smog situation, not a good day to be out in it, folks. Some of the stories we've been getting sound just plain weird. But first, here's Betsy with the traffic."

"Hi, we're getting an unusual report from the CHP on the Santa Monica freeway, near the Pico off ramp. Traffic is dead stopped, apparently due to a series of flat tires. One trucker who called in said that there may be as many as a dozen cars blocking the freeway, some with more than one flat. Sounds like some vandal, or a corrosive chemical spill, so watch out, and avoid the area if you can."

Rubber crack depth indeed, he thought. Now

there's a reproducible technology for you.

They headed up Bundy at ten miles over the speed limit.

"Why the hills?" she asked. "I can feel the pressure lessening already. His gaze is less intense."

"Air pollution simulation models divide the airshed over Los Angeles into a series of boxes, with all the information in the box averaged together. The model would 'see' the hills as having a single average height. So we keep dropping in and out of focus. Also, he'll have trouble controlling the winds up in the hills. The flow is channeled and uneven."

"But down on the freeways . . ."

"There's probably a line source submodel in the thing. It would keep track of local effects near roadways."

"The belly of the beast," she said absently, then as the thought occurred to her, "What about major intersections?"

He thought for only a second. "Best not to risk it," he said.

"Then hang on," she told him, jammed the accelerator and screamed right onto Idaho.

They used Westgate to cross both Santa Monica Boulevard and Wilshire, running two red lights in the process. Peters wondered about the police for a few moments, then decided that a reckless-driving citation was the least of their worries. Joella used Kiowa to get them back to Bundy and soon they were into the Brentwood Hills.

Charles King: Six Miles From Downtown Los Angeles

At some time in the past, the hilltop had been cut flat, presumably in preparation for construction.

Whatever the project, millionaire's home, corporate headquarters, or religious institute, it had proceeded no further, owing to high interest rates, the stock market, personal or organizational finances. Some pioneer vegetation had begun homemaking on the flat surface and the access road was still barely usable. Otherwise the place was nothing but a flat rock pedestal.

It was now the site of a conjuration.

The gathering numbered five—two couples and a leader—according to alchemical directives. The five sat at the five corners of the pentagram to provide foci for the elements of the conjuration, earth, air, fire, water and ether. Identical bell jars filled with the relevant substances stood before each of the participants.

The jar representing ether, evacuated to the hardest vacuum which the university physics department had managed to prepare, stood before the leader, Charles King. He stared into its depths, trying to clear his mind, listening for the biofeedback tone that would announce his conquest of the excitement that he felt for his most ambitious project.

In the early sixties, King had taken a degree in parapsychology from Duke University and had moved to California to begin his academic career. But all too rapidly a mood of academic stagnation had overtaken him. When psychedelia struck he was more than ready for a prolonged bout of drugs, philosophical speculation, and mysticism.

Not to mention the sex part.

But after the running-amok phase, and the commune phase, and the ego-disintegration phase, and other wanderings far afield, he still had not found what he sought. So he drifted back toward academe, trying to locate a scientific basis for all the magic that he had witnessed, whose substance still eluded him, whose reality he sometimes doubted.

Then one evening, in blackest despair, trying to blot out his consciousness with vodka and hashish, a blinding flash of insight brought him to a clarity and sobriety that he had not experienced (he suddenly realized) in years. His error had been to try to study magic, to bring it within the scientific paradigm. He had been trying to bend it to his will and to make it the slave of science.

But what if one went at it from the other direction? To hell with scientific tests of efficacy! To hell with statistics and papers for the journals and rational proofs!

Don't use magic as a topic for scientific study; use the fruits of science to assist the creation of magical phenomena.

The pentagram within which they sat was perhaps the most perfect pentagram ever constructed. It consisted of a single beam of light, multiply-reflected and returned to the helium neon laser cavities (five of them) that maintained it.

Each participant was connected to a polygraph and thence to a microprocessor. As each heartbeat and breath cycle approached unison, the hum in the small headset grew louder. And each of the five began to vocalize that hum, the harmony growing.

At the appropriate time (known by intuition, the ocean calls it forth), the hum is replaced by a chant, a mantra of invocation, syllables of power from the great books of devotion, the *Koran*, the *Book of the Dead*, the *King James Bible*, other texts, obscure and arcane. Occasionally, the effort of the chant would disrupt the unity of breath and heart and the participant would begin again to seek the basic tone. No matter. There is time, yet there is no time. There is only *now*.

Five individuals, seeking to become one, stared into the void and sought a Presence.

Awareness had come to Charles King and his

coterie sometime in early June. All of their various methods of divination had shown signs, powerful signs, not requiring any of the various statistical tests that Charles used to try to separate wheat from chaff. *Something* was out there, suddenly, large and looming.

When the smog started, they had begun to suspect.

So now they called to it. Who are you? What is your name and purpose? Give us a sign of your nature.

The flame in the bell jar flickered; the air-filled one emitted a low pitched tone. Static grew in their headphones, but they tried to ignore it, tried to accept it, tried to continue the link.

And then the sound of breaking glass.

Charles King sat immobile. He could not move or perhaps he did not dare. Even when he saw the fire engulf one of the five. When the air grew black to smother the next. Water became fog, acid fog, and a man screamed, though not as loud as the one who had his flesh blasted from his bones by wind-driven sand and glass. Fire. Air. Water. Earth.

The jar in front of Charles fell into shards, slowly, as if it were simply tired of holding the vacuum within. He watched it almost without interest, as one watches a bad movie late at night on TV. The self-aware portion of his mind judged that he was in shock. But awareness still lingered.

All sound left him and his skin flashed cold. He knew that he was now surrounded by vacuum, that he had only a few moments left to live. And in those last few moments, several things occurred to him.

They had called to something and it had heard them and had indeed given them a sign of its true nature. Its nature was death and perhaps there are indeed some things that man is not meant to know.

All of his life he had searched for such a thing, the forbidden knowledge. He had tracked it and analyzed its trails and spoor, or so he thought. And yet when he considered his card-guessing experiments, and dice-throwing, and remote-viewing, and all the rest, when he considered all the phenomena that had convinced him, and all the statistics and clever methods for wringing drips into his bucket, and then when he compared it to a thing that reached down and killed like a tiger stepping on a gnat, he realized that he had been looking in the wrong places and he had found nothing.

And one final insight was given to him before the roaring in his ears claimed him and that was this: their conjuration was elaborate and unnecessary. Anyone could ask the same questions they had asked and receive the answer: Death.

And many more would die before night fell.

Friday Evening

The evening sun was sinking down into the layers of brown, its light so attentuated that one could stare into it with the naked eye. With the waning light the intensity of the smog began to abate. The car radio informed them that five air-quality monitoring stations in the south coast air basin had that day recorded ozone levels in excess of one part per million of air.

He shook his head. "That's the highest I've seen it outside of smog chambers." He paused, unable to judge her comprehension. "Smog chambers are laboratory vessels for making artificial smog."

"Yes, I know," she informed him. "Raymond told me of their use."

"What else did Ray tell you? You used the name Haagen-Smit in your little incantation. Is that the proper way to ward off smog demons?"

She grimaced. "Ray told me a number of things about smog and its history. I do not remember very much of it; I lack the education to be able to listen intelligently in so technical a field. In a moment of crisis one uses whatever comes to mind. Haagen-Smit is perhaps a name to conjure with in smog?"

It was his turn to wince. "Yeah, you might say that. He discovered it—after a fashion. He was a Dutch perfume chemist who took a whiff of the air in Los Angeles and decided that he smelled oxygenated hydrocarbons. He also remembered a Swiss patent for oxygenating hydrocarbons by irradiating them in the presence of nitrogen oxides. So he repeated the experiment and *voila*—artificial smog. Why was your chant in German? Does it make it more potent?"

She looked at him with a tired smile, and shrugged. "I don't know," she said, and for a moment he thought he could detect the faintest lingering trace of a Bronx accent. "German is the language of chemistry, yes. Besides I don't know Dutch. Have a heart; I'm making this up as I go along, the same as everybody else."

"But you spoke of magic. You say that you are a witch."

"My sign says that I am a psychic reader. It even bears the picture of a palm, though I seldom resort to cheiromancy. The pay of a psychic reader is better than that of a lay analyst."

"It sounds at least as honest as contract-consulting work," he said wryly.

"Thanks," she said. "Ray said something like that once. Then he told me that it was just short of an insult."

"Ray was always so tactful."

"I was not interested in his tact," she said and that hushed him.

"Look," she said. "I said that I was a witch and I do not lie. I cast spells, I exorcise demons. These things can be done, given the correct interpretation of 'spells' and 'demons.' When I speak to a client, I speak to him with the voice of his mother or father or some other symbol of authority that he will obey. I can assume such a persona—that is a very lowly level of magic, yet it is a most powerful technique.

"This may seem trivial to you, parlor psychology in an occult guise. It is not. At deeper levels the unconscious mind is pure magic. And the effects are not limited to the individual psyche."

"You mean parapsychology?" he asked.

She grimaced. "No, I do not mean card-guessing and dice-rolling. I have looked at those phenomena and they are nonsense. They are scientific self-deceptions.

"Magic has no overt physical effects. 'Mind over matter' is not its essence. Mind over mind is much more important. But demonic possession is a real occurrence; to explain it as schizophrenia is merely trading one label for another. I have known people who had hexes cast upon them. That the casting was not thought of as magic did not change the pain of the victim or my treatment of it.

"But this," she said, indicating the smog heavy night sky. "This is beyond my experience. It frightens me."

"You spoke of a smog demon," he said. "You drove one away with German doggerel."

"Yes," she said. "But I do not know what I did or how I did it. I am attuned to perceive demons. I have never before seen one without a person attached. Yet I felt a presence and no one was there. My methods of divination all warn me of trouble from Raymond. Raymond is dead and still they warn me."

"All your instruments give crazy readings," he muttered, remembering his time at SCAQMD.

"Eh?"

"I was just remembering something I read: 'Hell is

where all of the instruments are perfect but none of them work,' " he said.

"One might say then, that we have entered a corner of Hell."

"Ain't it the truth," he replied.

Offices of the South Coast Air Quality Management District

Andreson flipped through the sheaf of memoranda in front of him and swore softly to himself. But not softly enough that Meyers, with whom he shared the cubicle, could not hear.

"Oh yeah?" opined Meyers.

Andreson just shook his head. "It doesn't pay to take a vacation. You lose a sense of the obvious. What's the first thing *you'd* do if the worst smog episode in history happened while you were in charge?"

"No fair," Meyers replied. "I know what they actually did. They recalibrated all the instruments."

Andreson shook his head again. "Assholes," he muttered.

"Look," his cellmate said reasonably. "There are mitigating circumstances. Just two days before 'Big Daddy' hit, there was an article in the L.A. *Times* about how effective recent smog control measures had been and how we hadn't had a stage-two alert in two years."

"But that was just luck; the weather's been good."

"Yeah, you know that, and I know that, but it makes good copy, especially if you maybe have running for congress in the back of your mind, like a certian highly placed person that I could name, but shan't."

"Yeah, but . . ."

"Furthermore," Meyers continued, "the measured smog levels are *mighty damn* high. High enough to maybe make someone think that the data is a little screwy."

"Oh, come *on*! Not all of the monitors at once. Not when you can look outside and see all hell breaking loose."

"Hey, don't look at me. I just work here. I'm just trying to explain the workings of this mighty machine that we call smog control. I am but a mere cog, trying to apply grease to a squeaking . . ."

"Oh, shut up," Andreson said in disgust. He paged through more memoranda, while Meyers sat smirking at him. At length Andreson tossed the papers back down on his desk.

"So now what?" he asked Meyers.

Meyers shrugged. "Word has it that they're going to try some emergency measures. They're dusting off all those things that they tried during the 'eighty-four Olympics: staggered work hours, temporary reduction of refinery throughput and electric power generation, you know, the usual bullshit."

"Think it'll do any good?"

"If a good Santa Ana comes up and blows it all away, you know who'll take some credit. Otherwise . . ."

"Yeah?"

"Ever piss in the ocean?"

Friday Night

Douglas Shreiber was a man with a high degree of self-awareness and almost no self-consciousness. Since this is almost the precise inverse of the usual situation, most people found him very difficult to understand. As one who had built his own merry-go-round for the express purpose of grabbing the brass ring, he was very aware of both his good fortune and his great talents. Being neither conceited nor overly humble, he was invariably mistaken for either one or the other. Such a constant exposure to the misconceptions and misperceptions of others, on so personal a level, made him tolerant of all human foibles. He didn't ask that his acquaintances be right, merely entertaining.

So Shreiber had an open mind armored with skepticism. His strong opinions were seldom voiced and frequently changed with the acquisition of new information. He was equally polite to parapsychologists, ufologists, mystics, computer scientists, and cosmologists. He was seldom given to snap judgments.

"That's crazy," Shreiber told Peters. "You've cracked from the strain and you are crazy."

"I hope you're right," Peters told him. "That would be a nice tidy explanation and I could use a nice tidy explanation. So I'll tell you what. I have a terminal and a modem upstairs. I'll get it and set it up. Then you can try to log into Macgregor's files. Only I will leave before you try, because I don't want to go through that again."

Shreiber looked at him intently. Peters's skin looked sunburned; his hair was lighter than it had been that morning. There were blond streaks in it. His clothing had a speckled look to it, as if he had been spattered with a cup full of chlorine bleach.

"I don't suppose that you were at the beach today?" Shreiber asked him. Peters shook his head. "And this isn't a practical joke either?" Another shake.

Shreiber looked around the room. "Somebody turn on the television," he said.

A wall panel opened and a screen appeared. The gathering then listened to tales of the smog emergency. One channel had gone into full-time news coverage. In places, the newsmen stated, smog levels exceeded measurement capabilities. Scientific authorities were baffled. Advice and directives were issued by the appropriate government officials. All of this was interspersed with camera shots of the night sky, where odd flashes of light could be seen.

"Chemiluminescence," said Peters. "Ozone reacts with various compounds to emit light. At concentrations of a few percent with carbon monoxide, it can cause a blue flash."

A newscaster interviewed a doctor, a female neurologist.

". . . complaining of tachycardia and angina after regaining consciousness," she said. "We had eight cases at one time in the emergency room, all from a disco on the Strip. My first diagnosis was overindulgence in amyl nitrite or any of the related compounds that have become fashionable. All of the patients claimed to have been innocent of such indulgence in recreational drugs, at least for one hour prior to the incident. I don't think that it was self-administered, but I do believe that they are suffering from nitrite poisoning."

"So what do you think was the cause?" asked the reporter.

"One of the men said that he had been attacked by a whirlwind," she said. "I don't know whether to believe him or not."

Shreiber looked at Peters. "That's getting pretty fancy," responded Peters. "Smog contains quite a number of organic nitrates and nitrites as trace contaminants. All of them are vasodilators—they drop your blood pressure and give your heart a kick. So the smog monster cooked up some heart stimulant specifically for some disco fanatics in bad need of a rush."

Shreiber walked over to the television and switched

it off. "Let's talk hypotheticals," he said. "How bad could this get, assuming that your insane surmises are correct?"

"How bad is 'I don't know'?" asked Peters. "How bad is deadly?"

"I don't want to believe you," said Shreiber, shaking his head. "So that means that I'd better." He looked over at Monica. "Would you please go into the cellar, look in the deepfreeze, and take out the large canister marked 'RAT POISON?' Inside you'll find a green can with turkish coffee in it. And set the water to boil, too. This may be a long night."

It was a long night, and Peters was not up to it. He was too tired to think; after about an hour, he could no longer respond intelligibly to questions. Shreiber sent him to bed.

Sometime near dawn he awoke disoriented and aching. It was several minutes before he could remember who he was.

"Hello," said Joella, who knelt beside the bed.

It was a small shock; he hadn't known that she was there.

"How long have you been there?" he asked.

"Not long. Only a few minutes. You cried out in your sleep."

"Was I very loud?"

"No," she replied. "I was the only one who could hear you."

"I am all right," he said.

"I know. I only came to be with you for a while."

"I'm flattered," he said. "But I don't . . ." His voice trailed off.

"I have been downstairs speaking of magic," she said. "It seems a very lonely thing. Discussion places a thing slightly out of reach. Sometimes that is safer than confronting it."

She lay down beside him. She held him gently. A

feeling of warmth and tenderness engulfed him.

"Even the whitest of magics is manipulation, the bending of persons and events to one's will. It is far too easy to become hardened from it. To begin to use others to one's own ends. To make the power an end in itself. I had progressed farther along that path than I realized. Farther than is comfortable to remember. My time with Raymond made that clear to me. We used each other, I think. And I think that in the end, he bested me at my own game.

"Magic requires power to work it. The symbols must be enfused with energy; the nature of the energy determines and is determined by the nature of the spell. Either side of the great polarities may be used. Love and hate. Pleasure and pain. Sex and death.

"Raymond's last accomplishment was to work a spell of death. A spell more powerful perhaps than anything since the age of miracles, if such a time truly existed."

She held him tighter. "If I wished, I could pretend that necessity dictates my actions. I could tell you that it is essential that we provide ourselves with the power that pleasure and sex may yield.

"But the truth is that I want you for myself and for no other reason. I refuse to consider other reasons. I saved your life and you seem kind and gentle, once one looks beneath your prickly skin. And I am frightened. And I must *stop talking*!"

She kissed him. And then they made love.

He awoke many hours later, with the angry red sun high in the sky. And he could not be sure that he had not dreamed the dawn.

Saturday Morning

Wilson Carver was a man who was finely balanced between the positive and negative aspects of life. He was either plodding or methodical, depending upon who made the assessment. Likewise, where some found him lacking in imagination, others saw a well-developed skepticism and a refusal to be led astray by wild flights of fancy. Intelligent (overly given to abstraction?), conservative (hide-bound?), well educated (intellectually rigid?), Carver would present a difficult problem of categorization to someone in need of pigeonholing their fellow men.

To his own credit, Carver himself was not given to making such value judgments either about others or himself. If pressed he would probably have said something like, "Well, um . . . I'm pretty sure that I do my job, um, well enough. Surely that's sufficient?" And he had few complaints about others, as long as they did their jobs.

Today his job included the care and feeding of a contract monitor, Major David Stern, USAF, who supervised several of the contracts that Carver's research group were performing for the air force. The pair had just left the low pressure smog chamber that was used for the air force high altitude experiments. Carver was showing Stern several of the other chambers that the research group was using. It was unusual to work on a Saturday, but Stern was on a tight schedule.

"For experiments at atmospheric pressure," Carver said in his slow, almost-a-drawl. "We don't require a, um, rigid structure. So we use these, uh, teflon bags, pretreated with, ah, ozone to deactivate the surfaces still further. We've been experimenting with photolyzing, uh, chlorine, as a deactivating agent, and that seems to work better than . . . ozone, even."

Stern broke into the slow-moving monologue, eager to speed things up and perhaps show that he had been reading the monthly reports that they'd been sending him. "So with the bags you just take out the air samples and let the bags deflate, rather than diluting the interior air?"

"Um, yes," said Carver. "There still seems to be some, ah, exchange, with the outside air, especially for, uh, low molecular weight compounds that . . . perhaps they diffuse more easily through the bag. It's not a large effect . . . it's maybe a factor of, oh, four or five below dilution. But we're trying to characterize it."

By this time the pair had passed through the large double doors out into the courtyard. A much larger bag crouched on a wooden platform above the dry brown grass. Stern indicated it with his chin. "Another teflon bag chamber?" he inquired.

"Um, yes," replied Carver. "This one is for a captive air study that we are performing. We had been running a series under another contract, uh, the purpose was to try to, oh, get replicate experiments both inside under, um, artificial lighting, and . . . outside under natural . . ."

One of the other researchers waved at him breaking his train of thought. Carver said, "Excuse me," then ran over to the small shed which housed several analytical devices and a stripchart recorder. The two researchers made puzzled motions with their hands and heads, then Carver returned to stand beside Stern, giving occasional sidelong glances at the bag and instrument shed.

"Probably trouble with the instruments," he said, his voice a bit puzzled and the first hint of agitation entering his speech. "We stopped the series to try these captive air studies. Somebody suggested that there was some 'X factor' in the air that is causing this anomalous smog lately. So we trapped some early morning air in the bag and we're comparing it with a synthetic mixture that we're familiar with. We have the bag divided as you can see, so if there is any difference like that that would be caused . . .''

Suddenly there came a popping noise from the shed, then a hissing mixed with various profanities. Carver broke off and ran to check on what was happening. By the time he reached the door to the tiny building the hissing had stopped and the other researcher was motioning him away.

The two researchers rejoined Stern. Both seemed to be intent upon a length of rubber tubing.

"The damnedest thing," the other researcher was saying to Carver. "We got a couple of odd spikes on the stripchart, like maybe we got back when we were using an unshielded line and the workmen would turn on a power drill or something. I was trying to decide whether to recalibrate when all of a sudden the seal on the chemiluminescence detector went; we probably dumped ethylene all through the shed and maybe contaminated the irradiation bags as well. Look at this; I've never seen anything like it. This tubing is just rotted away. What could do something like that?"

"An 'X factor,' maybe?" suggested Stern.

Carver looked at him as if suddenly remembering that the other man was there. He smiled faintly. "Let's not jump to conclusions," Carver said. "More like somebody spilled some, um, reagent of some sort and then was too embarrassed to report it. Or possibly . . .''

He never finished the sentence. While the three men had been intent upon the traitorous tubing, the right side of the divided bag had grown cloudy and had begun to bulge. With a startling *whumph!* it burst and its contents spilled forth.

A nearly opaque white cloud for an instant caught the sunlight and flashed a rainbow of divided light at the awed trio. A pseudopod of mist touched the other side of the teflon bag and with another *whumph* the cloud grew. It swooped to the analytical shed and the small wooden construction exploded into flame at its touch.

The noise and heat jarred the three men to life. Carver yelled, "Fire!" and ran to an extinguisher affixed to a nearby wall. His co-worker disappeared into the larger lab building and reappeared moments later with a firehose unwinding behind him. "Turn on the water!" he yelled at Stern, motioning toward the building. Stern broke free of his paralysis and ran through the door as the sounds of the hissing CO_2 extinguisher reached him.

In his haste Stern managed to cut himself on a bit of broken glass while turning the valve on the firehose. His curse was cut short by the scream from outside. He looked out the window to see Carver, obscured by the mist, clawing at his face. Then the extinguisher exploded, smashing him against the burning wall of the instrument shed. Carver's body rebounded, crumpled and lay still.

The other man yelled and dropped the hose, whether to run to Carver's aid or to just run was unclear. In the next instant the monster had caught him as well; there was a sudden sharp opacity and the man and his clothing burst into flames.

Stern raced outside and caught the firehose as it snakewove its way across the yard. He sprayed water at the burning man long enough to extinguish the blaze and then tried to direct the water stream at the burning building. He held his breath, wondering if he were about to die.

The firehose came apart in his hands.

He was drenched in an instant and as he turned to try to make it back into the larger lab building, the shredded firehose writhed beneath him, alive from the uneven pressure of the water as it escaped from a thousand leaks. He tripped over it, unable to keep his footing on the now muddy ground. From his vantage point on the ground he saw flames leap up from the roof of the main lab, and he heard the explosions from inside, the numerous canisters of calibration gases and hydrocarbon samples yielding their contents all at once.

He saw the white cloud give one final swipe at the burning building and cave in the roof. Then the cloud moved up into the sky, blurred, and was gone. Stern managed to roll over, onto his hands and knees, and crawled away from the building. He was far enough when the building collapsed so that only a few cinders reached him.

Late Saturday Morning

Peters took the time to shower before he went downstairs. He didn't shave. His skin felt raw and parched. Maybe I should grow a beard, he thought randomly. His little voice queried, just in time to have it go prematurely white? He grimaced.

As he walked down the stairs, Peters heard Monica's voice. She was talking into the phone at the bottom of the stairs.

"Hello, Mike? We need some info, fast. Can you put out the word? What we need is not exactly on the up and up. We need everything you can get about EPANET, the operating system, security measures, the works. Up to five K for anything useful, and if anybody knows how to crash the system we'll go up to fifty. What? No, don't ask, best to not know. Can you query some of the pirate nets? I've already sent something out on Pirates Cove and Hackers Haven, but there are some new ones, yes? Wait a sec, let me get a pen. Okay. Hole in the Wall, International

Binary Movement, um, and Amnesty. Any more?
Check for us, all right? Your check is in the mail.
Catch you later.''

Monica looked up at Peters. "Hi, Walter. Everybody else is already up. My work assignment is de-
foliation. Can't talk now." She picked up the
receiver and began to dial again.

The lower floor was a hubbub. Ben was setting up
a small computer with a phone line connection. On
yet another phone, Larry was directing logistics for
people yet to arrive. Joella and Shreiber were covering several blackboards with strange symbols and
arguing. Vaguely familiar people scurried back and
forth on undiscernible missions.

"No, of course we can't be sure that human
psychology applies," Joella was saying. "But if it
doesn't then we are not going to get anywhere."

"I'm not disagreeing," Shreiber said. "It is just
that I'm not sure we need tie ourselves to any one
system of explanation. In fact, we may get more
mileage out of cross-references. Anything that shows
up in several schools of thought is more likely to be
true. It's a matter of how we do the matching." He
turned to Larry. "Can you call Franks at Harvard? I
seem to recall hearing of someone's thesis that involved conversion of Jung's *Man and His Symbols* to
Boolean algebra. I thought it was a stupid idea at the
time, but we can't really rule out any methodology at
this point. Hello, Walter, welcome back to the unreal
world."

Peters smiled weakly and accepted Joella's em-
brace. "So what's on the agenda for today?" he
asked.

Shreiber shrugged. "Reconnaissance. Joella and I
are trying to formulate a theoretical structure for the
interaction of magic and physics. Monica and Ben
are putting together everything we know about the
EPANET. Maybe we'll come up with a safe way to

query the system. Larry is rounding up the extended family. We're trying to evacuate everybody who we don't need to try to solve the problem—get them out of L.A. Or at least get them here, since this seems to be some sort of safety zone.''

"It's mostly the hills," said Walter. "We're also near the top of the modeling region, where boundary effects become a confounding factor."

"Mmm, yes," said Shreiber. "Joella mentioned some other possibilities, too. Anyway, Larry is going down to the CAPRI center to try to retrieve some of the papers that you and Joella had to leave so hurriedly. We need as much information as possible about Macgregor's researches. Do you think that a visit to his home would prove productive?"

Peters nodded. "Yeah. Ray was a workaholic. He kept a personal library of technical material at home even when he was in school."

"Can you arrange to examine it?"

"I suppose I could call Meg. She'd probably have a key. Then I. . . ." His voice trailed off and he shuddered. Joella reached out and took his arm.

There was a lull in the general activity. Monica had hung up the phone. Ben turned and looked at Peters. Shreiber motioned him to sit down.

Monica spoke first. "What's wrong, Walter?"

Peters took a deep breath and looked at Joella. She nodded. He held out his hand in front of him. There was a tremble to it.

He said, "My mouth is dry and my hand shakes slightly. Someone is having a late breakfast in the kitchen; I can smell the pancakes. I don't give a damn, because I have absolutely no appetite. These are all symptoms of the activation of the sympathetic nervous system: Fight or flight. An objective observer might conclude that I am scared shitless."

Shreiber nodded. "An understandable reaction. It is, in fact, quite dangerous for you to go back into the valley." He scowled. "But I know of no one else that we can send. We need Joella here, and she would not know what to look for. Also, I am not sure that she would get much cooperation out of Macgregor's wife."

"Walter must not go down there alone," stated Joella flatly. She pursed her lips. "Monica. May I speak with you privately?"

Monica raised her eyebrows slightly in puzzlement. "Of course," she said.

They went to the breakfast nook, a small room adjacent to the kitchen. It smelled of blueberry pancakes and the violets that grew in a windowbox. Joella closed the door. She turned to Monica.

"You and Walter were lovers," she said.

Monica's jaw went down a quarter of an inch. "What has he been telling . . ."

Joella cut her off. "He has said nothing. But I know. That is the nature of my talent. It is important that you understand. You must accompany him. You can serve as a shield and a warning. You will be able to tell when the monster's gaze gets too close.

"You will be able to feel it through Walter," she said. "It hates him. It wants his head on a spike. If you feel that there is someone angry at him, if you feel hatred but there is no one there, run!"

"Can't Walter feel it?"

"He needs someone to feel it for him."

Saturday Noon: The Great Man

Smog comes in two varieties, oxidizing and reducing. The latter is sometimes called "London smog," although they do not get it anymore, not since they banned the burning of soft coal in home furnaces. The sulfur in the coal makes a sulfuric acid mist that

*gives atmosphere to Sherlock Holmes stories and
killed some five thousand people in 1952.*

*Oxidizing smog is called "Los Angeles smog," for
obvious reasons. More often it is called "photochemical smog" because it is the result of a chemical process initiated by sunlight. Under the influence of
ultraviolet light hydrocarbons undergo a slow oxidation process. The molecules break into pieces which
absorb oxygen, then pass some of the oxygen over to
nitrogen oxide molecules, forming nitrogen dioxide.
The nitrogen dioxide absorbs light, breaking down
into an oxygen atom and the original nitrogen oxide.
The oxygen atom combines with O_2 to form O_3,
which is ozone; the nitrogen oxide continues on its
way.*

The Great Man sighed. They were behind schedule
on the book, *Photochemical Smog: Observations
and Theory*, and this section was a prime example of
why. The graduate student who had written it simply
had no understanding of the proper tone for a text-
book. His style was too chatty, too folksy. Not that
the Great Man was a prig. The Great Man had a real
appreciation for informality. In person he was folksi-
ness personified. But there was a difference between
a lecture audience and the academic community who
would be the ones to respond to the book. Anything
less than utter seriousness of style and . . . well, they
just wouldn't take it seriously. No sales, no royalties.
Perhaps that was overstating things a bit. Indeed, in
all modesty, anything with the Great Man's name attached would be accepted. But it would not do to
undercut the professional tone of the endeavor.

It was too bad really. He'd had hopes for this particular grad student. Not only was he technically pro-
ficient and smart, but he seemed to be one of the few
that the Great Man had encountered with any feel for
English; most of his students seemed to treat it as a
foreign tongue. But maybe this student (what *was* his

name anyway?) had some ego problems about bending to the appropriate conventions.

The Great Man sighed again. The book wasn't what was really bothering him, he knew. He was preoccupied by two things, the air outside his window and the contents of his lower desk drawer. He bent his thoughts to the air in an effort to forget about the lower drawer.

He got up and went to the window. It was the only window in the entire building that could be opened. Rank had its privileges. He unlatched the frame and pushed it open. He could feel the warm distasteful air mix with the cool air of his office. He looked up into the ugly sky.

What's going on? he thought to himself. He had lived in L.A. for thirty years and he had never seen it like this. And it was inexplicable. The word frightened him. Inexplicable. And he was supposed to be the explicator. Inexplicable. Not in thirty years.

He wrinkled his nose. It didn't even smell like it was supposed to. He wondered what Haagen-Smit would have said, his friend with the educated nose. Oxygenated hydrocarbons? Yes, that might be true. But more specific. Banana oil? Gasoline? Ah! Acetaldehyde perhaps.

The next breath of it was so sweet-smelling that it nearly choked him. His head swam. He hurriedly closed the window. The smell followed him back to his desk. He picked up the papers that he had been working on and tried to read. His hands shook. . . .

He carefully put down the papers and moved a paperweight to rest on them. He rose and walked over to a file cabinet. He pulled open the top drawer, rummaged around for a bit, then removed a key. Back at his desk, he sat down and unlocked his bottom desk drawer.

He placed the glass in front of him and uncapped the bottle. "I'm sorry, Toni," he said as he toasted the picture of his wife. Then he poured the fine amber liquid down his throat. It didn't burn much. Not really.

Early Afternoon

The door opened. "Hello, Walter," Meg said. Her voice was husky. His eyes had not yet adjusted to the dark interior, so he could not clearly see her face, but he could tell she had been crying.

"Hello, Meg," he said. He embraced and kissed her. "This is Monica," he told her. "I had an accident yesterday and it's a bit unsafe for me to drive, so Monica is chauffeuring me around."

Meg looked at him and nodded. His scorched and abraded face certainly bore out his story. So what if the accident didn't involve a car, as he had implied? It was the literal truth.

"Ray's work stuff is in the backroom," she said. "I've been sorting through some of his things . . ." She looked as if she were about to cry again.

"Do you have anything to drink?" Monica asked. "The smog today is really hell on the throat, and I could use something cool. I'll help you fix it."

Meg looked at Monica and smiled, grateful for the interruption of whatever had been her tearful train of thought. She tood a ragged, almost gasping, breath.

"Of course," she said. "I'm not being a good hostess, am I? The kitchen is over here."

To the sounds of ice cubes clinking and drinks being poured, Peters prowled around the living room. Macgregor had been a book junkie and Peters scanned some of the titles in the bookshelves. Science fiction and fantasy. Heinlein, Asimov, Bradbury, Leiber. Arthur C. Clarke and James Branch Cabell. Philosophy. Neitzsche and Max Stirner. *Secrets of the Samurai. Karate Is a Thing of the Spirit.* Books from *Scientific American* on biology, geology, and the evolution of the solar system. Carl Sagan. Freud and Jung. The *I Ching.* A book of Jackson Pollock prints. The biology of spiders. A mishmash.

His eyes lit upon one book, lying on its side and out of place: *Dog Soldiers.* He picked it up and flipped through it. A line caught his eye: "The pellet with the poison is in the chalice with the palace." He fought down a sudden sensation of vertigo.

"Hey, Walter," Monica called out in one of her brashest tones. "Do you want cranberry or grapefruit?"

"Both," he answered. "Mixed."

The arrival of the iced drinks saved him further brooding. Monica always had that knack, to cut through, to control a mood. He took the glass and drank half its contents in one long gulp.

"I've been going through Ray's stuff," said Meg. "I got a little weepy, I guess. I left the back room alone, though. That's where he kept his office. You haven't said what you're looking for."

Peters shrugged. The question made him uncomfortable. "Ray was working on something to do with acute smog episodes—like the one we're having now. It's got everyone baffled, so if Ray had any kind of handle on it . . ." His voice trailed off.

She looked at him intently. Her stare transfixed him. "You are one of the world's worst liars; you always try to blend it in with the truth, but the seams show."

She got up. There was a nervous energy in her motion. "I made a little pile of our stuff, Ray's and mine. I'll leave now so that you can go about your business."

She disappeared into the bedroom, to reappear a moment later carrying an overnight bag. She seemed to be, if not angry, at least determined.

"Good-bye, Walter," she said as she opened the door. "Call me sometime, if you get the chance. It's nice to have met you, Monica." She did not slam the door as she left.

Peters blinked, dazed by the abruptness of her departure. He looked at Monica.

"What . . ." he began, but he could not think of the question. Monica cut him off with a wave of her hand.

"This is one of those times, Walter. If you have to ask, the answer won't do you any good."

The Manse

Shreiber erased the blackboard, shaking his head. "We're getting bleary," he said. "Time for a break."

In the kitchen, Shreiber sipped coffee and tried not to think about cigarettes, while Joella nibbled absently at a roll.

"Worried about Walt?" Shreiber asked.

"Some," she said. "Wondering about him as well. He contains the key to much of this, and I need to understand him."

She looked at Shreiber. "I need to understand him for my own reasons as well."

Shreiber looked at her and nodded. "Have you come to any conclusions yet?"

"He suffers from winner's guilt," she said.

Shreiber raised his eyebrows. "Ah," he said. "That's very good. I appreciate your witchcraft more with each passing hour. 'Winner's guilt' is a very good description of Walter's affliction. How did you make your assessment?"

"I know of no specifics," she said. "I know generally of events that can cause such a thing."

"Such as?"

"Bad luck to one's family, friends, and peers. Envied good fortune. Seemingly effortless accomplishment. Those with inherited wealth often feel guilty about the very existence of poverty.

"But most important, some people call up insecurity and fears in others. They hurt other people just by their superiority. If they care for people, it hurts them. If they try to avoid the pain by shutting out the world . . ."

Shreiber nodded. "A double bind," he stated. "That's quite an analysis for so little information. You may be too good at that sort of thing, you know. You must frighten people yourself."

She nodded. "That is one reason why I saw it so clearly in Walter."

He bit his lip. "Walter's family was not wealthy but they were affluent. I believe that he did always have the sort of effortless talent and intelligence that does make people feel uncomfortable.

"Walter once told me of a friend of his in school; I think his name was Scott. Scott and Walter were always, not so much rivals or even competitors, but whenever there was a competition, an examination or an essay contest, the two of them would be one and two, trading the top spot back and forth.

"Walter was not as likable as Scott; much of Walter's present affability is hard won skill. At that time . . . well, Scott was voted 'most likely to succeed' in their high school class. He then proceeded to have a psychotic breakdown during his first year of college. I think he's a postal clerk somewhere now.

"Walter had a roommate in college who attempted suicide three times. He didn't leave school until Walter moved out."

"He was using his own pain to attack Walter," Joella said flatly.

"I think so," Shreiber said. "I've seen it happen."

"Walter cares for people," he continued. "But his attitudes and opinions are very much out of the ordinary. He has an original and unpredictable mind. It's unsettling to many people. His very existence causes them to doubt their own beliefs. Then to have him sail through life with such apparent grace and ease . . . The doubts grow acute."

"And Walter knew Raymond," said Joella.

Shreiber nodded. "Walter left school after he had completed the research for his Ph.D. dissertation, but never wrote it up and presented it. He told me he just got sick of academia. Having lived that life myself, I'm not surprised. His tolerance for pettiness is even less than mine.

"Walter and Macgregor were working for different advisors on the same project, the continued development of a large urban photochemical model for the Environmental Protection Agency. Macgregor's approach was quite academic: highly refined numerical computation schemes, a complicated and cumbersome chemical kinetic mechanism. Walter spent his efforts on clever simplification and run-time optimization—the engineering approach.

"So Macgregor published first, got four or five papers out of it and received his Ph.D. Walter took his version of the model with him, refined it to the point where it could operate on a minicomputer and joined with a consulting company in San Francisco. The two models gave basically the same results, but Walter's took about one-tenth the computing time and was easier to use. The company marketed it to state air pollution agencies and Walter made a lot of money."

"And Raymond hated him for it," said Joella.

"Did he ever tell you that?"

"No," she said. "But I knew Ray."

Prometheus

The monster grew. Its need outstripped its growth.
Its appetites outstripped its need. It hungered.

The measures used to thwart its feedings were puny
tactics, of little consequence were the monster not
already lean and ravenous. But who dares snatch
food from the feeding carnivore? Who pleads with
the feasting wolf? Who will tease a tiger?

A refinery in Culver City shut down half its operations. An irritation. The Redondo Beach power plant
cut its load by sixty percent. An anger. Sections of
the Santa Monica and San Diego freeway were
blocked off. The monster began to rage.

In one of its lesser incarnations it swooped down
upon a freeway interchange and ripped the fuel from
several of the metal creatures cruising there. In the
aftermath of the feeding, traffic blocked and yet
more food was to be had. Yet these were morsels
only. Insufficient.

The beast turned its attention to the high places,
where perception was difficult. There was food here
also; it came in slow trickles during the heat of the
day.

During the heat of the day. . . .

The smog devil coalesced into a whirlpool of
smoke and exothermic reactions. If it had eyes, they
burned with the rest of its form, hot and dark. Its
claws caressed the sagebrush and chaparral. The
branches smoldered, fumed, then burned. The smoke
lifted toward the sky. The devil gorged upon it. It fed
within the blackness. Its happy cries echoed for miles
and gave waking nightmares to those with ears to
hear.

Late Saturday Afternoon

"What's this?"

Monica looked across the room at Peters and flipped a postcard at him. He snatched at it, missed, and looked ruefully at her as he bent to pick it up.

He read from it, "Hello—We're now holding these books/mags for you: *Between the Night and the Golden Dawn*—A Change of Hobbit, 1853 Lincoln Boulevard, Santa Monica. Phone (213) GREAT SF. Best, Sherry. Never again."

He looked at her. "Never again?" he asked. She shrugged.

She said, "It's on the way home; we could stop off. Are we finished here?"

He looked down at the pile of books and papers at his feet. It was everything that they could find that might be of significance. Some notebooks, a few reference works, loose papers and a card file. Not a very large pile at all.

He made a sour face. "Aw, hell," he said, shaking his head. "Let's get out of here."

On the way out to the car, Monica sniffed and looked up into the hills, squinting at the shadows of the late day sun.

"What is it?" he asked.

"Smoke. Probably brushfires in the hills."

> *I see your hair is burning,*
> *Your hills are filled with fire . . .*

Travel was slow going. The radio moaned out some old Doors tunes while they tried to circumnavigate the tie-up caused by the partial shutdown of the Santa Monica freeway. With all the traffic forced onto the surface streets, even the side roads were jammed. And they had to use the side roads. The main roads were too visible to something malign. . . .

It took more than an hour to go ten miles. At times the smell of smoke was strong, blending with the bite of smog. The shadowed hills sometimes showed a glimmer of a smoldering glow.

"Damn and double damn," he muttered. "Now the bastard has a new toy to play with. He's discovered fire."

> *If they say I never loved you,*
> *You know they are a liar . . .*

A Change of Hobbit

They parked next to a car with well-aged Grateful Dead bumper stickers and walked around to the front of the building. Daylight was dying; it had to be near closing time.

A Change of Hobbit was bigger than he expected. It was most unlike the bookstores Peters frequented in San Francisco and Berkeley. The decor assaulted him with color, blue ceilings rainbowed down to a brown rug whose color was not a monotone, so it jangled on his tired eyes. One of the doorways was arched and actually did have a rainbow painted over it, reminding him of the tunnel entrance to Marin County just across the Golden Gate Bridge from San Francisco.

Finally something clicked and he recognized it as a perfect L.A. bookstore, big and roomy, noticeably lacking the clutter of stand-alone bookshelves. Instead, there were tables with artwork, sculptures, and models of movie sets.

There was one four-foot-long shelf of nonfiction.

"Hi, I'm Sherry. Can I help you?"

The woman's voice had a tinge of Jewish brass in it and Monica automatically developed a faint New

York accent. "We'd like to pick up this book, if we might."

Sherry looked at the card and scowled. "This card was sent to Ray Macgregor." She looked at Peters. "You're not Ray. You're not bad, but you're not Ray."

Peters stared back at her, noting a faint glint in her hair, some sort of mild dye tint that showed as a ghostly peacock eye. Her scowl had turned into a friendly smile. He did not smile back.

"No," he said. "I'm not Ray Macgregor. Ray is dead. He died of a heart attack three weeks ago."

Sherry's face clouded. "Oh hell," she said and turned away from them. After a deep breath she turned back. "I liked Ray," she told them. "Otherwise I'd never have . . ." She looked down at the card again and made a face. "This damn book is just bad luck."

She came out from behind the desk. "Oh, well," she told them. "It's back in my office. C'mon with me."

She headed back toward the rear of the store, detouring around a lunar landscape model in the back room. "I liked Ray," she said as she walked, "and he sweet-talked me into this. The books he wanted weren't the kind we usually carry. We don't do searches for occult books or anything like that. This one was borderline; some sort of occult fantasy written by a Japanese follower of Anton La Vey, privately printed in San Francisco, very rare and just godawful, from the looks of it. But there were supposed to be some kind of magic rituals coded into it, so we get weirdos in here asking for it. Ray was the first guy to ask about it who didn't look like a candidate for the booby hatch."

She opened the door to her office. There was the faintest lingering scent of marijuana smoke inside.

"Here it is," she said, picking up a battered

leatherbound volume. "I just glanced through it. It's very hard to read. The type is funny and it's broken up with a lot of Japanese lettering. Frankly, I wouldn't have tried to get it at all except that I know a guy in San Francisco who's good at searches and Ray paid me upfront. Tom, the guy who found it, is laid up with a broken leg now, and he tells me that the store he found the book in just had a water-main break nearby and lost almost all of their inventory. I'm not massively superstitious, but . . ." She shrugged.

"Here," she said. "Let me get a bag for this . . ."

As she spoke there came a sighing sound that filled the room, a room which suddenly seemed clouded with a faint blue mist.

Monica gasped, her eyes wide as she whirled and grabbed Peters's shoulder, ready to shove him to the ground, out of the path of . . . what? There was no onrushing car, no obvious attack, just a whispered moan that came from nowhere, and the sound of dry paper amid windblown dust.

Sherry gave a little shriek and dropped the book. It struck the floor with an oddly muted sound. "It bit me," she said in a frightened voice. Monica reached out her toe to prod at it.

The binding of the book crumbled to yellow powder at the first touch. The book collapsed in on itself, pages flaking, visibly aging as they watched it.

All three of them started to speak at the same time but were interrupted by a yell from out in the store. They hurried out to find a disaster.

The fate of the occult text had not been singular. Every book in A Change of Hobbit had met the same fate. Paper dust and book jacket shards, oddly discolored, sifted from the once full bookshelves like cheap sand dunes in a B-movie. The store clerks and the few remaining customers gaped in astonishment.

Sherry looked around in puzzlement and disbelief.

"No," she said emphatically. "This didn't happen. I'm going to go home and have a hot bath and some smoke and blow and it's just an ordinary day and this didn't happen."

She called to one of the clerks. "Bill? Call my insurance rep. I'll see him tomorrow. Everybody go home. This didn't happen tonight. Pack up and close it. Go home. That's what I'm going to do."

She turned to Monica and Peters. "We don't do searches for occult books. You hear? We never, *ever*, do searches for occult books!"

Saturday Night

Mike the bartender had a lot of things on his mind this evening; plenty to worry about. But if he had to list them it was no contest as to what was number one. It was that guy drinking down at the end of the bar. He'd been there since the previous shift, starting off on beer, but he was doing harder stuff now, and something about the way he was just sitting, drinking and watching the TV gave Mike the creeps. Mike had to glance over in his direction every thirty seconds or so to make sure that the guy hadn't pulled a knife or something. Those were the sort of vibes he gave off.

Damn. It wasn't as if there weren't enough other things to worry about. Business was great, if you could call wall-to-wall people great. The tips were okay and several of the customers had been pretty generous with their cocaine earlier in the evening. That seemed to be the way things were going the past few days, lots of liquor and lots of coke. It made sense too. It was the smog. Booze and coke got rid of the scratchy throat and itching nose and eyes at least temporarily and temporary relief was about all that you could expect. And try not to think of all the stories that you'd heard about glowing dust devils or clouds of thick smoke that seemed to wander about purposefully, looking for something or someone.

No, people went out, got drunk, picked up a stranger (or made a pass at the bartender), got into a fight, whatever, all to avoid thinking about it. These were just not normal times.

He looked over at the end of the bar again and froze. The guy's knuckles were white from clutching his glass so tight that Mike was glad it wasn't a wineglass or it would break in his hand. There was a nightstick located strategically beneath the bar and Mike moved over to keep it within easy reach. The guy looked like a bomb ready to go off and Mike was sorry he hadn't asked him to leave earlier.

What the hell was eating him? Mike wondered. He seemed to be staring at the TV. Mike stole a glance but it did no damn good. It was just some pizza commercial. He looked back at the guy just in time to see him lay out a five dollar bill, get up and leave.

Whew. Mike sighed inwardly and relaxed. There was going to be trouble somewhere tonight, he was sure of it. But not here, not in his place. And these days, that was about all you could hope for.

By the time they reached the car, Monica was shaking. Peters reached out to touch her shoulder but she flinched at his touch and pulled away, leaving him with his hand awkwardly outstretched. Monica walked hurriedly around to the other side of the car but she didn't get in. Instead she put her head down onto the cool metal of the roof and let her harsh, ragged breathing slowly subside. Only once or maybe twice did she allow a sob.

Presently she straightened, took a deep, deep breath, and looked over at Peters. "Let's go," she said, yanking the door open with such ferocity that

Peters feared for the hinges.

Monica started the engine and pulled away without bothering to allow a warmup. The first few gear changes were rough and she seemed to welcome the need to pay close attention to the quirks of the balky car. At the first red light she turned to Peters, staring at him intently, as if trying to see into his skull.

"What is it?" he asked.

"She was right, wasn't she? You didn't feel it."

"Feel what?" he asked.

"Yeah," Monica said decisively. "You didn't feel it. If you had, you'd know what I'm talking about. The hatred in it. The rage. You can't possibly know how much that thing wants you dead."

He said nothing as she pulled away from the light. When she next spoke, her voice was softer, almost dreamy.

"I didn't really believe it until now, you know. It was just another role, another grade-B sci-fi flick. Sometimes it's giant ants. Now it's smog. Who can get upset over smog? It can't crawl into your bed and bite you. Say something, dammit! Don't leave me alone here!"

The sudden change caught him by surprise. "Uh . . . what?" he said helplessly. "Are you okay? I know you've just had a shock, but . . ."

"Oh, but me not buts, and I withdraw my request. Maybe you should just shut up instead and let me blather.

"Don't you understand? I believe in your god-damn smog monster now! I didn't before. Nobody can who hasn't seen it, felt it at their throats. How the hell can you believe something like that? It's too goddamn weird! It's like quarks, and ufos, and bird creatures from Sirius, and nuclear war, and the planet Neptune. You can only pretend to believe in them, learn your lines, do the scene and then go back to the real stuff like sex and drugs and new clothes, being late for work or out of a job.''

"Monica, I . . .''

"Didn't I tell you to can it? I know I'm raving but I'm goddamn lucid and I know what I'm saying and I know that, that *thing*, in a way that you never will if one believes your new girl friend, and all of a sudden, I think that I do. She's absolutely right. It wants your head on a pike and your guts strewn down Sepulveda. But you're just the one at the top of its list, and it has a very long list. And you have to kill it. Walter, damn you, you have to kill it!''

They were cruising at about sixty in a twenty-five mile zone, but the streets were nearly deserted. Peters tried not to show it, but Monica felt his tension and slowed to a saner speed. She seemed to relax.

"I'm sorry, Walter. That wasn't called for. I'm just a crazy lady after all. I'll be okay by the time we get back to the house.'' She looked at him briefly and sighed.

"But what about you? Will you be all right? Can you dodge this thing fast enough and still fight it? How's your *ukemi*, how're your rolls, can you take a fall and not be too shaken to still fight?

"Poor Walter. You always did like a challenge. The hard problems were the only ones that ever kept your interest. Well, you've got a doozy now. Think you're up to it?

"Tell me, Walter. How are you going to kill a dead man?''

Midnight: Marty Williams

Watching television, how's that for a job? Counting the goddamn ads.

Marty made the entries into her logbook and flipped the channel. The sponsors pay to have the ads run, but sometimes people screw up. The tape gets accidentally degaussed, the midnight-to-six engineer dozes off, so the agency spotchecks. Keeps people on their toes and sometimes gets refunds, or more likely some free airtime.

So that was her job. Come to glamor city and wind up counting ads for nostalgia records and pocket fishermen in the early morning hours. But it was better than sleaze-joint waitressing and she'd had to do worse things than *that* a few times. And it let her stay at home with the kids.

One more ad to count, then, thankfully, sign off. This one was a bit of a pleasure though. It was one of Trina's. Well, Trina and six other kids singing some deliberately off-key song about an amusement park. Then fireworks, then the national anthem.

Good. Finished. She slapped the logbook closed, then winced, afraid she'd woken one of the children. But no, just sleep sounds came from the bedroom.

She dimmed the living-room lights and looked into the bedroom at the three beds. She smiled. Then a little shiver went down her spine. She knew the feeling. *Good luck doesn't last.* Pure habit. So many hopes had been killed over the years. But maybe this time . . .

She forced her thoughts back to optimism. The smog was really screwing up business. The roads were a mess, she'd heard. Doug and Monica had told her that everybody should stay at the Manse until it blew over, and boy, had they ever collected a crowd for it. There must be over a hundred people staying at the big house. She was just happy that everyone was letting her and the kids alone. There was some talk of trying to evacuate all of the kids in the place, but . . . ah well, don't worry about that. Maybe the smog would end soon.

The agency had called yesterday. They'd had several inquiries about work for the kids in just the past week. One of them was maybe even for something that wasn't commercial work, but the agency man cautioned against getting one's hopes up. Nobody had movies dropped into their laps.

"There's a lot of fly-by-nights out there, you know," he'd said. "And something about this one didn't ring true."

Marty shook her head. The little shiver touched her spine once more.

Early Sunday Afternoon

Throughout the night and morning people had been arriving at Shreiber Manse. Family, friends, friends of family and families of friends, Doug and Monica had alerted the network of the dangers. All who couldn't flee the city were taking refuge.

The group also constituted a brain trust of sizable power. The problem that confronted them required solutions artistic and magical as well as scientific. No other group was so well suited to the task and certainly no one else was so truly alerted to the danger nor so prepared to believe in things impossible.

By noon, the population of the Manse had passed one hundred, a slight strain on the foodstores, but space would not be a problem until twice that number. The aftermath of one spectacular party had seen over three hundred hungover souls fight off the light of day (total attendance was said jokingly to have required scientific notation to state). By the time the smog emergency reached its crisis, the gathering at the Manse would again approach that number.

A little after noon, Douglas Aloysius Shreiber gathered thirty of the Manse's swelling population into the grand ballroom. He had always been good at lecture.

"Most of our portable think-tank is here now, so I'll bring you up to date. Monica and Walter have retrieved what they could from Ray Macgregor's personal effects. Joella's reference material is on its way, as is what's left of the contents of Macgregor's office. Larry and Johnny are out doing some legwork trying to get more of a handle on Macgregor. As I'll explain later, any insight into Macgregor's psyche and state of mind during his last months of life is likely to be important, so we're trying to contact anybody who knew him, co-workers, girl friends, his martial arts instructor and fellow students, that sort of thing.

"It's going to be a bit crowded here for a while but we are pretty far out of the central L.A. basin airflow, and Walter says that it's as likely to be safe here as anywhere in southern California, with the warning that we do make it more dangerous by trying to fight this thing. So we're also looking into getting a safehouse of some sort, or maybe a combat command post.

"If what Walter and Joella say is true, and I do not believe they are lying or insane, then this whole area is in danger. Monica corroborates the smog demon experience and you've all heard the wild stories on radio and TV, so we'll take the strangeness of the situation as a given. There is literally no way of knowing how bad this smog will get unless we find some way of tapping into whatever it is that caused it. The current hypothesis is that it is magic, whatever that means.

"I am trying to ascertain what that does mean, with the help of Joella and whatever research material she can supply. Walter is our smog expert; we are hoping to guess the nature of the phenomenon by contrasting it with scientific plausibility. Which is a snooty way of saying that we know it's impossible, but what we want to know is *how* impossible.

"We have established one thing to my satisfaction. We need to know its name. This is clear from both a practical and a symbolic standpoint. You cannot control a demon unless you know its true name; we cannot gain access to Ray Macgregor's computer files until we know the password.

"Walter suggests that a failed attempt is very dangerous.

"Joella insists, and I tend to agree with her, that we must treat this smog thing as if it were alive. Certainly it shows many of the characteristics of life, especially growth and irritability. Other than that I have no opinions. Believe what you will, it can kill you, so be careful.

"As for the plan of action, well, wait'll you get a look at this one. We're going to try fortune-telling and meditation. I know that that sounds weird to some of you, even to those of you who are used to occult demonstrations. But we haven't much in the way of other ideas.

"So here's the deal: we've set up a shop of some sort in every room of the house. Yes, it's going to be séance night here at Shreiber Manse. Choose your scam but don't be afraid to mingle. Just remember, we're after the monster's name. If anything interesting comes up, write it down and get it to me. I'm going to try some information-theory techniques on it.

"And if you believe that bullshit, stick around, it gets worse."

The Martial Arts

"Hello. Yes. You wished to speak to me? If not too long, we may speak. Did you enjoy the demonstration? I, myself, am of two heads about it. It is showing off and so is not discipline, but we must have publicity for the school, yes? And the breaking of bricks with one's bare hands is very popular, so we do it—to please the crowd. Not much of a crowd today because of the bad air but we must try. The true purpose of our art is hard to demonstrate, so we must show the breaking of bricks rather than the molding of the self.

"What was it that you wished to speak to me about? Raymond Macgregor? Ah, yes. I knew him. No, it would not be fair to speak of him as my student. I taught him little, a few *kata*, nothing more. He already had his direction before he came to me.

"I believe that he came to us primarily because we had a heavy bag. Does that seem strange? But he was dedicated, you see. He would come in and stand before the bag for an hour, deep horse stance, striking the bag with his left hand only. Then he would do a *kata* and return to the bag for an hour using his right.

"The other students would sometimes make jokes about him. Some of the other students. The temporaries, the ones who will quit in six months. They want immediate enlightenment. They wish to be able to break a brick. They paid their money, they want the tricks. They want cheap magic. They make jokes.

"My other students, the ones who have been with me for a time, the ones who have at least a glimmer of understanding, they did not laugh. They were a little afraid of Raymond, I believe. Not for fear of being made a punching bag; they had nothing to fear from Raymond in the physical or technical sense. But they feared his intensity, his focus, his magic.

"There *is* magic to it, you see. It can steal souls as well as save them. But one must go through much physics before one reaches the magic.

"How can I explain? Ah, example: the showy thing, the breaking of a brick. Many things happen simultaneously. The opposite arm is pulled in toward the center. This adds to the torque on the hips. The striking arm likewise is turned; taking advantage of the additional extension which this allows. The hips turn slightly, and the center is lowered, again adding to the power available. For one brief instant the diaphragm is tensed, transmitting the force of the entire body, and preventing muscular shock, 'having the wind knocked out.' The tension is released in a deep cry. This helps provide the focus and it scares the shit out of your opponent.

"During the instant of the cry, all of the power of the body is directed from the hips through the torso and arm to a focus between the second and third knuckle of the hand. It can break a brick. It can kill. But neither of those things are its true purpose. It is a tangible concentration of the will. That is its purpose.

"My school is Korean-style. Punches, not chops. Tae Kwon Do and Hapkido. Straight lines and circles. The lens is circular, the convergent beam is of straight lines. The circle and the line both devolve to the point. The focus. The magic.

"Raymond had all the focus that a man could want. He could break a brick or build a house. But he did not know what he wanted. He wanted the magic. He could not understand how much of it he had. He did not understand where it came from. He was blind to it. So it grew wild in him. I was a little relieved when he stopped coming. It pains me to admit this. But he was too much for me. I would have had to send him away. With more training he could have killed. I do not think that he would do so, but I think that if he were going to do it, I would not have been able to stop him."

In the skies above the city, the monster grew.
It no longer looked like smog; the billowing clouds

of noxious gases blotted the sky and turned the daylight to a dingy red. The sun was lost behind the swirls of evil haze. At night the sky lit with chemiluminescent flashes casting multiple shadows and giving headaches and waking nightmares to those who stared at them for too long.

The city was paralyzed. The roads were clogged with abandoned automobiles, their fanbelts, waterhoses, and tires rotted away in the oxidizing air. A state of civic emergency had been declared. All nonessential travel had been banned. The national guard swept along the arterial routes that led away from the urban sprawl, trying to clear the way for the evacuation of those least able to stand the smog. Asthmatics, emphysemics, those with heart disease, all were urged to appear at evacuation sites where they were herded into air-conditioned buses and sent out along those roads that remained open. Few people managed to reach the evac stations; most preferred to huddle indoors, trying to cope as best they could.

Stories of "killer whirlwinds" multiplied. Some told of abandoning a car to see it dissolve into corrosion. Others told of strange crackling noises heard just before a grisly death. Small explosions had been reported; no one knew of their significance.

Arthur had first met Beth after a demonstration of judo and kendo in the park. He first noticed her while he was in the middle of a sword *kata*. Afterward, he contrived to be leaving the area at the same time as she.

"Hello," he said to her. "Are you a dancer?"

She smiled at him. "I've studied dance for about ten years now. How did you guess?"

He grinned. "Elementary, my dear . . .?"

"Beth," she supplied.

"Elementary, my dear Beth. Your legs. They are well developed with highly defined muscles. Bicycling tends to favor the thighs over the calves and your proportions are different. Running will develop the legs to such an extent, but it does nothing for overall coordination and grace. In fact, I have found most runners to be a bit stiff of movement, whereas your walk is fluid and a pleasure to watch. The only things that I know of that produce both muscle development and a graceful movement are tai chi, aikido, and dance. Since I know most of the martial arts practitioners in the area, I guessed that you were a dancer. Ta-da.''

"Well, I guess you win the Sherlock Holmes award,'' she said, still smiling.

"Well, perhaps, we can come up with a suitable prize. Are you busy?'' She shrugged in answer.

"Well, are you hungry, then?'' he asked.

"Yes,'' she replied.

"Good,'' he said. "So am I. Just give me a chance to change my clothes in yon convenient men's room and I will take you to lunch.''

She looked at him in amusement. "Are you always this forward?'' she asked.

"Hell, no,'' he said. "Usually I'm shy and tongue-tied.'' He raised his wooden practice sword, his *bokken*. "It's the influence of the *bushido*,'' he said. "Put a wooden stick in my hand and I become a gate-crashing barbarian. *Arrgh!*'' he yelled, and made a sweep with the sword, and pretended to cut himself in the groin.

Beth broke out laughing and their friendship was assured.

Apart from a mutual interest in things physical *(that* part of the relationship was consummated at an early date), Arthur and Beth shared certain spiritual leanings. She had studied Kundalini yoga for many years (yet another hangover from the sixties, was the way she described it). Arthur had come to a similar consciousness by way of zen and *bushido*, the way of the samurai. So they taught each other their favorite postures and mantras, and became soulmates as well as bedmates.

Thus it was only natural that, when it came time to make the attempt at meditational espionage at Shreiber Manse, Arthur and Beth would set it up.

In the main music room of the mansion, Arthur hooked up a white noise generator to drown out any exterior distractions. Next door was an anechoic chamber left over from a failed attempt at a home-re-cording studio. The conical foam-covered walls swal-lowed up all sounds. The lights were dimmed in both rooms. All actions were to the same purpose, to elim-inate distractions for those who meditated.

Throughout the rest of the mansion, other techni-ques were being tried.

Sunday: Shreiber Manse

The time was early evening, when the monster napped.

"How are we doing?" asked Peters.

"I'm not sure," said Shreiber as he drained the dregs of his coffee. "There's a lot of funny stuff, and it seems to suggest something, but there's nothing really definite, yet.

"There's a lot of reference to the sun and to de-struction, no big surprise there. Maybe the smog beast is a part of some sun god myth. Those are plenty powerful.

"Anyway, the tarot readings have shown the Sun crossed by the Tower three times so far. That is heap big bad news. Those all had a nice little association with the Hanged Man, once inverted, which means a bad experience, which we might not learn from. Pleasant.

"The *I Ching* did a nice little pirouette. *Chen* to *Shih Ho* to *Li* and then back again. That's Thunder to Fire by way of Biting Through. Lots of misfortune and close calls in the moving lines. Li, incidentally, represents the East."

"In Macgregor's library," began Peters, "there were a few occult texts that I gave to Joella to decipher if she could. The only other interesting things were martial arts texts, a few books on Japanese folklore and a 'learn Japanese at home' record."

"Do you think that we could be dealing with a Japanese symbol-type then? *Between the Night and the Golden Dawn* was supposed to be linked to Japanese ritual magic, for all the good an unfindable book does us. That would explain the references to the East. Also, it would make sense that the tarot would have less in it than . . . Oh Lord, I can't be saying these things, can I?"

Peters said, "Sure you can. Just keep saying to yourself, 'Nothing is more bizarre than mathematical topology.' "

"I did lousy in topology," said Shreiber.

"Well there you are, that proves . . ."

There came a yell from the second floor. The two men leaped to their feet. The yell came from the stereo room. "What happened?" asked Shreiber as he burst through the door. The electronic waterfall swallowed up his words. Arthur was holding Beth tightly in his arms. She seemed to be struggling in a loose, disjointed way.

"I don't know," said Arthur. "Beth and I were trying candle meditation, when all of a sudden she started to hyperventilate. When I touched her she convulsed. She's getting better though."

It was true. The shaking stopped and Beth's breathing began to slow. After a few minutes some clarity slowly returned to her eyes.

"What happened?" she asked.

"I asked first," said Shreiber. "What is the last thing that you remember?"

She blinked. "Well, I was looking at the candle . . ." she began, then as her glance locked back onto the flame, her eyes glazed over and her breath became a rasping gulp.

"Look out," said Arthur, "she's doing it again." He put his hand in front of her eyes and shook her gently. Her muscles relaxed and she gave a little sob. Shreiber knelt beside her.

"Don't worry about it, Beth. Just try to relax. Walter, blow out that damn candle."

Peters did so and then looked to the people who had clustered at the entrance to the room. "Go next door and tell the others to stop the attempts at meditation. It looks like it's too dangerous. Somebody get some sleeping pills. Phenobarb, if you can find it. It's used for treatment of epilepsy and I think that it might be a good thing if Beth slept for a while." Shreiber nodded his agreement.

As they were descending the stairs to the first floor, Monica met them. "We've got something, I think," she said.

"What is it?"

"The Ouija board. We were getting nothing but the usual bullshit, until Aiko sat down to it. Then it started into a long hymn to the goddess of the sun and the god of thunder. On a hunch, I got Keiko to join Aiko at the board. It spelled out 'shura,' said 'good-bye,' and we haven't gotten another word from it since."

"What is a *shura*?" asked Shreiber.

"It is a type of Japanese hobgoblin. A 'vengeful spirit.' They live in the sky and do nothing but fight each other and anything else that gets in their way."

"Oh, Christ!"

"My feeling exactly."

"Well, how the hell are we going to find out the

name of some Japanese vengeance. demon?'' asked
Peters.

''I have an idea,'' said Shreiber.

They assembled the group.

''Through the good and brave efforts of Aiko and
Keiko, two friends of ours from Monica's jujitsu
dojo, we have some good evidence that the smog
beast is Japanese in character and thus probably has
a Japanese name. How to find it is the puzzle.

''We are now going to try a variation on the 'four
deep.' Four deep is a type of wordgame invented by
Claude Shannon, the information theorist. It is used
to explore the semantic structure of language. In the
version that we normally use, four words from the
middle of a grammatical sentence are written down
and the first word is covered. The next person in the
group makes up a sentence containing the three visible words and writes down the next word. The second
word is then covered, and the three visible words are
passed to the next person in line and so on.

''We are going to try a Japanese ideogram variation of this technique. Monica has set up several
easels with blank drawing paper downstairs in a
dimly lit room. The drawings can be covered with
several cloth shrouds. Up here, we have every Japanese text that we can find, including several nice
books of Japanese calligraphic art. So look through
the ideographs to try to get a feel for what they look
like. Then go downstairs, take a brush and make a
mark that best joins up to what marks are visible.
This will be something like a reverse Rorschach test,
because afterward, we will get Aiko and Keiko to
look at the results and see if there are any legitimate
Japanese characters to be found. If there are not,
then we will raise the level of context, that is to say
we will leave more and more of the paper uncovered
in each succeeding round. Eventually we should get

something out of it. With any luck, what remains will have some bearing on the matter at hand, since it will have been filtered through the sum of our unconscious minds."

The assembled gathering set to it.

"This had better work," said Shreiber to Peters. "Meditation is too dangerous and the other things seem too general. What next? Augury? We're fresh out of chicken entrails."

Monica took command of the project, happy to be of use doing something other than brewing coffee and keeping the perpetual buffet going in the kitchen of Shreiber Manse. She had no personal or political aversion to playing domestic, but she had been uncomfortable at being left out of the action.

And the real action centered on Shreiber, Peters, and Joella, no doubt about it. The three of them were in a perpetual huddle, trying to blend their varied skills in order to piece together a plan of action from information that was disconnected and disjoined. Peters and Joella even slept together (was her opinion of that entirely positive, she wondered?) and Shreiber seemed to have reverted to the sleepless frenzy that had been his work pattern in the days of commodities and random-walk algorithms.

Now Monica had a role to play and she played it well. She had commandeered the easel and brushes. She undertook the task of covering and uncovering the canvases and showing each person the proper way to make the calligraphic stroke. And above all, she distracted everyone, to allow the release of the unconscious mind.

Her efficiency masked fear. Several times since the smog had begun, she had dreamed of her judo class. Each dream ended when a faceless student whom she had never seen before was transformed into an armored warrior and began to kill. His sword was flame and each victim died without a sound.

She remembered nothing of the dream when she awoke. But she felt an urgency to the task before them. They had to know the devil's *name*.

"I think we are getting close," she told the kitchen think-tank. "The patterns are beginning to look like ideographs."

"That's good," said Shreiber. "It's only a beginning, you know. I suspect that we'll need to know more about the nature of the specific computer program that fleshes the beast before we can do much against it."

"Can't you just pull the plug?" asked Monica.

"Unfortunately, no. There isn't even a plug to pull. The program is on a distributed network spread out over hundreds of machines."

"We are also dealing with one tough bastard," said Peters. "I've called up a few contacts in EPANET administration. They inform me that there is no record and no billing to Ray Macgregor or CAPRI for this project. That sounds to me as if the program has gimmicked the operating system, it may even be part of the OS by this time. Which means that what we're trying to do may be at least as hard as crashing the EPANET.

"I've put in a few calls to friends who have a flair for this sort of thing. Our best bet is a computer scientist up in Berkeley who always had the reputation of being able to crash any system at will. Distributed systems are another kettle of fish, however."

Joella then spoke. "Have you noticed that the telephone system in Los Angeles seems to be passing unscathed? From what I understand, electrical systems in general are having a lot of service problems, but not the telephones."

"That's true," said Shreiber. "We've had to switch over to the household generator twice because of the brown-outs. The radio said repair crews have their hands full with the electrical grid, because of corrosion on the transformers and insulation break-down. Television stations go off the air frequently for the same reasons. But PacTel seems to be just breezing along."

"Well, sure," said Peters. "The monster could hardly be expected to attack his own nervous system. I'll bet that if we checked, we'd find that computers that are hooked into the EPANET are much less prone to breakdown than others in the area."

"Could we exploit that in some way, do you think? Maybe we could . . . no, that probably wouldn't work. Besides, if it had to it might just communicate to all its scattered parts magically somehow. Until we get a peek at its insides, we can't really plan any-thing."

"Speaking of which," said Monica, "it's time for another unveiling."

Williams

The cab dropped him off by the front gate. He waited until it was out of sight and walked around to the side wall. After climbing up the ivy to the top, he rested for a while and took another swallow from the flask that he carried.

He'd started out the evening drinking beer. He could not remember when he switched to the hard stuff. Probably during a commercial. They were enough to drive any man to drink. Goddamn kids.

He took another gulp. Where had this flask come from, anyway? He didn't remember buying it, either. No, wait, maybe he'd gotten it at the liquor store. No matter. The bourbon cut the nasty taste in his mouth and that was what counted. The benign vapors over-powered the smell of the smog.

He jumped to the ground, twisting his ankle

slightly when he landed. It didn't hurt much but he cursed his luck all the same. Sometimes the world was nothing but broken glass and chuckholes. A man had to be smart and hard to get through it all. A man had to insist on his rights.

He looked up through the trees at the sky where some of the brighter stars managed to pierce the haze. Weird colors though. Even here, nearly above all the damn smelly smog. And over toward the city, there was a hint of flickering lights in the sky, like aurorae. For some reason the sight of the sky made him angry.

He drained the last of the flask and threw it down. He headed for the rear of the Mansion. He didn't know why, but he was sure that Marty and the kids were back there.

The downstairs room was dim and no one thought to turn the lights higher. The tension was palpable; everyone staying at the Manse had long since passed the point of believing in the reality of the creature that they faced, though few would have been able to state the reasons for the belief. Their faith was compounded of some combination of nightmares and the nightly news.

Monica unveiled the canvases without fanfare. All eyes turned to Aiko and Keiko, whose eyes in turn stared at the crisscrossed expanse of white.

"Well?" said Monica and Shreiber, almost in the same breath.

Aiko laughed nervously. "After the times before, it is strange to have them be so clear." Keiko nodded in agreement.

"Over there is the symbol for smoke," said Aiko. "Like smoke from a fire. And the other is sun, of course."

"Sun-smoke," muttered Peters. "That's one hell of a good name for photochemical smog. How do you say them in Japanese?''

"Sun is *taiyo*,'' said Keiko. "And smoke is *kamuri*. *Taiyokamuri*,'' she said.

A sudden chill went through the gathering then, and Peters found himself looking around to check for any windows which might crack and break. Joella put her hand upon his arm to reassure him.

Upstairs, from the depths of a drugged and dreamless sleep, Beth moaned softly and then cried out.

The knock at the door made Marty start; she didn't have time to realize why, but the knock was familiar. The door was unlocked. A second after the knock the doorknob turned and the door swung open with a bang, leaving a dent in the cream-colored plasterboard.

It was Bill. (Oh God, Marty thought, he's been drinking!). "Get your things,'' he ordered, in that tone that she knew far too well. "We're leaving.''

"But . . .'' she began and immediately knew it to be a mistake. That tone was *no backtalk! Don't even try! Hop to it! Otherwise* . . .

He slapped her. Not too hard. Not as hard as he could have. Not nearly as hard as he could have. It just rattled her teeth.

"Leave her alone!'' It was Colby. He had something in his hand. It might have been a stick.

"Colby!'' she yelled. "Get out of here! Run!'' But the boy didn't budge. Then Bill hit her again.

This one was hard. Nearly as hard as any that she could remember. He used his fist in a roundhouse that caught her at the temple. The gray sparks flashed in her eyes and the next thing she knew she was sprawled against the couch, trying to force her legs to move, trying to make her voice work, trying to stop the horror.

Colby launched himself across the room, swinging

wildly with the broken broomhandle in his hand. The first swing connected with Bill's elbow and it hurt the big man, even through the liquor. The pair struggled briefly, then Bill shoved Colby across the room with all his might, boy and broomstick flying apart. Colby slammed into the wall next to the bedroom door. He looked at Bill, fear replacing the determination in the boy's eyes.

Bill sneered. "I've been trying to kill you since before you were born. This time I think I'll finish the job."

His words unlocked the few last drabs of strength that remained in Marty. She shoved herself at Bill, half leap, half stagger, and clutched at his waist.

"No, Bill, please honey. Don't hurt him. We can go somewhere. Away. We can go away." She tried to make her coaxings convincing. She tried to think of something to say that he would believe. Something that would break the berserk spell that the whiskey wove around him. But her despair told her that this time it was not going to work. This time nothing would work except the sight of blood. Hers, the children's, anyone's.

But her pleadings were cut short by a blur from the bedroom door. Anthony slammed into the trio, low, just beneath Bill's knees. (Had he picked up a few tricks from watching Monica at the *dojo*, Marty wondered dazedly?) The four of them tumbled to the floor and thrashed wildly about. A table overturned and the lamp crashed to the floor, flashing green as the bulb shattered. Now the only light was the dim illumination that peeked from the bedroom. The living room was a dance of shadows and silhouettes.

Colby and Anthony had scrambled free of the pile and had retreated to opposite corners of the room. Bill shoved Marty away and her elbow cracked painfully on the hardwood floor. Her moan of pain was barely audible. Bill looked down at his side and was surprised to see a trickle of blood. The broken broomhandle had jabbed into him during the scuffle and the jagged edge of it had made a bloody gouge. He reached down and picked up the offending piece of wood. He eyed it unsteadily, as if asking it to give an account of itself. Then he hurled it with all his might at the wall where several shelves held assorted vases, toys, books, and the clock radio. Vases crashed and the clock radio bounced off the wall shelf to dangle forlornly from the cord that was too short to let it reach the floor.

Several of the toys on the shelf began to move, windup toys that had been partly wound but quiescent, awaiting the jolt to bring them to life. The only other sounds in the room were the harsh breathing of the four combatants. Bill looked around the room wildly, trying to keep the other three in his gaze, trying to remember what he was doing, what he should do next.

One of the windup toys was spitting sparks; it kept advancing long after the others had wound down. The light from the sparks and the noise of the toy's advance kept pulling at Bill's gaze. He swayed slightly.

"Stop it!" he said at the toy. "I don't need any of your lip!" He chuckled to himself. He took a step and reached out to grab the toy.

He stopped. The sparks coming from the toy's mouth illuminated the spot of blood that remained on his hand from having touched the wound on his side. The toy stopped its motion. In the shaft of light from the bedroom Bill's face grew tired and he looked like he wanted to cry.

He picked up the windup toy and stroked its head. He held it out toward Marty. "Godzilla," he said to her and gave the toy's reptilian head another stroke. He wound the toy three times and put it back on the shelf. Sparks flew from its mouth as it walked away from him back in the direction from which it came.

Bill's arms sagged to his sides. His head slumped. "Marty, I . . ." he began, but he did not finish. He just shook his head.

She recognized this other Bill, the slump to his shoulders, the lost tone in his voice. She managed to find her feet and she went to him. She gathered him in her arms and led him to the couch and cradled him, rocking him back and forth, whispering soothing words to him, waiting for the others to come from the big house and take him away.

PART THREE

GODZILLA VS. THE SMOG MONSTER

Monday Morning

Pacific Southwest Airlines' Flight 63 from San Francisco International Airport (SFO) to Los Angeles International Airport (LAX) was one and one half minutes behind schedule. This fact was of no real importance, except for the theoretical implication of a three percent error in a fifty-minute flight. Only the air traffic controllers were aware of it, and even they didn't care.

The vice-president of Systems Research Associates fidgeted in his seat. He was an impatient man and had he known of the infinitesimal delay, he would have had an opinion about it. Instead, he squirmed slightly once more and wondered how quickly he and his colleagues would be able to get cabs, once they landed.

There were eleven employees of SRA on this flight; it had been something of a last-minute arrangement. Originally only three of them were supposed to be going. The occasion was a conference on long-term trends in Los Angeles air pollution. But L.A. was in the middle of one hell of a smog episode and consequently the attendance list had mushroomed. There was suddenly a lot of interest in smog once again, interest that even reached the highest levels of state and federal air pollution control bureaucracy. And that meant money. And he meant for SRA to have its share. They had to show a presence.

For the twelfth time he wished that they had been

able to contact Walter Peters. He was a star employee and he was already in L.A., but he seemed to have dropped out of sight.

They had begun their descent. The pilot said something about the smog and across the aisle RGI grinned at the remark.

The vice-president felt a bit annoyed at himself when he noticed that he often thought of people by their initials, as if they were corporations or international airports. He suspected that the SRA memo system, which referred to everyone by initials, had something to do with it. Sometimes, the vice-president was annoyed at himself for so seldom noticing the habit. The vice-president of SRA was a man with an active and imaginative conscience.

From back behind him somewhere came the voices of JPK and GZW, the chemists in the group. The two of them were professionally so umbilically linked that people tended to refer to them as "you guys" even when only one of them was present. Across the aisle from them SRH was saying something to TWT, probably a bad pun, and PDG craned himself over their seat backs to try to get his two cents in. The president sighed internally. Chemists and meteorologists, that was what most of smog science was about. And his boys were really good at it. Too bad none of them knew anything about making money.

Outside the window the first few brown streaks began to pass over the wing. The president shook his head and squinted at them. My lord, he thought to himself, it really is bad down here.

It was his last coherent thought.

The mythology of aviation has many names for the various devils that live to plague and harry and kill. Some speak knowingly of "air pockets." Others invoke "downdrafts," or "clear air turbulence." One devil with a large sect of worshippers is "wind shear," which may (unlike turbulence) be precisely defined provided the conditions are mathematically ideal. Which of course they never are.

Still, a part of the phenomenon is easy to understand. The lift given to an airplane's wings depends upon the speed of the airstream flowing past them. Under conditions of extreme atmospheric stability, the speed of the wind may vary drastically with height. Thus, if a plane is descending through such a wind shear layer, it may experience substantial variations in lift. There may be temporary vertical winds of some force—down drafts. And turbulence near the ground may result in a sizable momentum transfer to the air or to a solid object influenced by the air. This momentum transfer may be likened to a push or a shove. There are many ways to describe any phenomenon.

And here is another: somewhere in a place that is not a place because it existed in the abstraction of a computational net, a series of secondary abstractions mutated, changed. And in a somewhat harder abstraction that some intellectualize as a "flow field," an analogous series of mutations occurred. And a transfer of momentum was the result.

Flight 63 from San Francisco and all its passengers and contents were flung from the sky to break upon the land like a fragile toy smashed to the floor by some childish, petulant god.

The plane crash made the midmorning news, but no one at the Manse thought anything of it, just another disaster in the week's long litany. Maybe here were deaths that had nothing to do with the smog.

The first report to contradict that conclusion came at two P.M. A small feature story on one of the radio news channels noted the grisly details, that nearly two dozen smog scientists who had been flying in for a conference had perished almost as soon as their plane had entered the L.A. smog layer.

Someone told Peters. Later he could not remember who.

He called the offices at Systems Research Associates. The first two tries he got busy signals. The third time he got one of the secretaries, her voice husky with an edge of hysteria, not to be yielded to, but always just an inch away.

"Walter!" she exclaimed. "Are you all right? We can't get any decent news from down there and . . ." she broke off with a cough that may have masked a sob.

"I heard the news of the crash," he said. "Is it true? Who was killed?"

"Everybody!" she cried, and this time it was a sob. "Shep and Bill and Paul and Gary and . . . Oh Christ, I'm sorry, it's just that I've been on the phone all day. Family, clients, insurance men." She said the last words as if they were a curse. "But that's no excuse for going to pieces."

"It's okay, Diane," he told her. "I think I'm going to pieces myself."

There was a short silence at the other end of the line. "Walter?" Diane asked. "What . . . Is there anything that we can do?"

"Yeah," he told her. "Make sure everybody keeps away from here. Don't even let anyone come down here to claim the bodies. Tell them that I'll do it and that it's dangerous for anyone else to come to L.A. This smog emergency is getting worse and the authorities may have to evacuate, no matter what they try to tell anyone."

"But it wasn't the smog that caused the crash . . . was it?"

"Not exactly," he told her. "But if anyone asks tell them that there may have been some sudden visibility impairment and that it's not safe to fly into the airports down here. Tell them anything you like.

Just make sure they realize that they should stay away.''

"Walter," she said, a new puzzled tone to her voice. "What's going on down there?"

"Death," he said, and instantly regretted it. But by then he'd hung up the phone.

Then he was prowling the grounds, not aimlessly, there had to be some pattern to it, but he couldn't feel anything through the numbness. He felt like the silver ball in some pinball machine. There is a tree, rebound. Here's the tennis courts, rebound. No set pattern, just energy and reaction.

Where did the energy come from? He felt so tired. As if he hadn't slept in days. Maybe he hadn't. He couldn't remember. Late-night brainstorming merged with all the readings of Macgregor's notes and library and the trying to work it all into a digestible whole and the search for SunSmoke's name. . . .

They'd gotten it too. Maybe that was the problem. Optimism. They had been making progress. He'd begun to believe that they might actually win. Hope . . .

Dashed like a toy airplane. All his friends and colleagues. Who was next? The investigators' victories were measured in little snippets of information. Taiyokamuri won more permanent victories. He killed. Maybe that would be the measure of their final victory—to learn how they would die, just before the deed.

He was carrying a baseball bat. Another mystery. Where had he gotten it? From one of the play areas. Why had he picked it up? Don't even try to remember. You're in shock. Besides, it felt good in his hand. Solid. Not like air at all. Not like death at all.

In one of the many little used corners of the Mansion's grounds there stood a simple iron pipe frame that might once have supported a child's swing. It was set in concrete, two supporting pipes and another about shoulder height. Children climbed on it before the advent of The Contraption. Now its only purpose was to hang windchimes.

Peters carefully removed the metal and shell chimes and stood in front of the iron pipe crossbar. He took a swing at it with the bat. The wood gave a solid jolt in his hands and the iron pipe rang with the impact. It felt good. He liked the sting in his hands. He swung again, harder. And again.

And again.

And again.

After a time he began to cry. He remembered company parties, which he mostly didn't like, and picnics, which he did. He remembered hallway banter and trips to conferences. Screaming arguments over salaries and expense accounts and minor technical points in papers that never got published. The memories filled him up and at the center of it was the utter and total emptiness of loss; of good times obliterated when the future died. And he sobbed his losses and whimpered and yelled and screamed. His hands became scraped and raw from the rubbing of the bat. When he noticed the pain, he welcomed it, held onto it, needed it. He let the blood mix with his sweat and the sweat joined his tears and he kept swinging at the iron pipe until the bat was nothing but a bundle of ragged splinters. And then he slid to the ground and lay there without moving for a time, neither asleep nor fully conscious.

Joella came and found him without having to search. She picked him up and he was surprised at her strength, that she could lift a grown man without noticeable strain. She carried him back to the house and laid him down on the living room couch and bandaged his hands. Everyone else kept away from them for several hours, while she stroked his head and whispered things to him that left no memory but which were kind and had so much comfort to them.

And then it was sunset.

"We can't stay here," Joella said.

Shreiber looked over at her where she sat with Peters' head still cradled in her lap. From time to time Peters would twitch slightly, or stir restlessly, like a child trying to remain asleep.

"I agree," Shreiber said. "I've made arrangements to move us to another house."

"Where?"

"Hollywood Hills. I own it. It's rented out but the tenants have evacuated. They're friends anyway. It's plenty big enough to hold our war party and it's high enough to offer some of the same kind of protection that this place does. Did."

Joella nodded. "The hills, the altitude, that was only part of it, protection against the smog itself. SunSmoke exists on many levels. The smog is only the outermost manifestation. On the more hidden levels, the emotional, the magical, the personal and psychological levels, we are becoming vulnerable."

Shreiber walked over to a fish tank that gurgled in a corner, strategically placed so that the last rays of the afternoon sun could find it. That time was now, and a shaft of light from the window fractured in the tank and became a rainbow on the wall. Shreiber leaned against the wall and studied the colors. They seemed oddly mottled to his tired gaze.

"Too many attacks," he agreed. "Beth, Bill Williams, this airplane business." He shook his head. "They seem so disjointed. Unrelated. Yet I'm sure they are not."

"SunSmoke cannot see us, so he is shooting blindly. And he is finding the range. A little while ago Walter was whispering something about acetaldehyde being under its spell."

Shreiber scowled. "It's a component of smog . . ." He thought a moment. "Oh Christ," he said in a weary voice. "It's part of the oxidation sequence of alcohol metabolism in the body. Alcoholics have unusually high levels in their blood. So, what . . . ? SunSmoke has particular powers over alcoholics? He winds them up and sets them off?"

Joella looked at him. "Bill Williams," she said.

He nodded again. "He just needed a little push." He touched the spectrum on the wall. "So what stopped him?"

"We had better find out," she said.

He straightened and turned to go. "I'll make arrangements for the move. Should we leave tonight?"

"Before dawn, I think. And . . . Doug?"

"Yes?"

"The hills were not the only reason for the safety here. The matters that we discussed earlier? About jealousy and resentment? How people so easily hate a winner?"

"I don't . . ."

"This place was a personal refuge for Walter. It was safe. Nobody hates him here."

They set out at midnight, the war party of scientists, programmers, mathematicians, and occultists. Everyone else remained at Shreiber Manse. With the war zone moved, those remaining were judged to be safe. Or as safe as anyone could be.

They followed a route carefully plotted through the hills that surrounded central L.A., monitoring the police emergency channels as they moved.

Earlier attempts by the authorities to control automobile traffic during the emergency had been a joke with no punchline. The smog itself had had more of an effect. Eventually, stalled cars blocking roadways, gas stations sucked dry by demons or demanding motorists, physical discomfort and fear had reduced travel by far more than official ukase. But authority maintained at least the pretense of command; roadblocks and checkpoints proliferated. Southern California, never a bastion of central control, was rapidly dissolving into enclaves and anarchy.

The caravan avoided several haphazard checkpoints and meandered into Trousdale Estates. Fire had cut a swath through the area and most of the inhabitants had evacuated.

"Do you think these things will work?" asked Shreiber. He tapped a metal cylinder that lay beside him on the car seat as he drove.

"I don't know," said Peters. "They should at least give us a few seconds grace if one of the whirlwinds attacks." He gestured at the gas mask that hung at his side. "Who knows if any of this stuff will work?"

"What's in them?" asked Shreiber, again indicating the metal fire extinguisher at his side.

"Powdered manganese dioxide, which destroys ozone catalytically; baking soda; phenol. Smog has a lot of acid gases in it; I'm hoping that the baking soda might disrupt those a bit. The phenol is a radical scavenger to try to upset the chemical balance that holds the devils together. It's all under pressure. I used your nitrous oxide tank to supply the propellant."

"It's nice to know that stuff is good for something. And if we hit fires?"

"Turn tail and run for it."

They avoided the fires but they saw not-too-distant hillsides alight with a charcoal glow. Twice they changed course because the police and emergency radio channels alerted them to wind changes and jumped firebreaks.

"Hey Doug!" The CB radio at Shreiber's side crackled with static.

"Yeah?"

"To the northeast. Water bombers."

Binoculars revealed a scene of surrealistic splendor —a series of B-52s strafing the hillside (already aflame as if napalm grew wild like a desert flower) with water, specially treated with detergents to increase its wetness. With each diving attack a cool dark spot would appear and the umber glow grew mottled.

"Can't see the bombers very well," said Peters as he stared into the binoculars. "There's too much smoke. I hope . . ." he broke off.

"What is it?"

"I'm not sure; trouble I think. Can we contact the . . . no, there wouldn't be time."

He picked up the radio. "Hey, Larry. Get your camera ready. Something's about to happen."

At the edges of the billowing cloud, an eddy of smoke detached from the greater mass, and huddled in upon itself. It was oddly shaped. No one could see that its true nature was a solitron, a complex wave whose curious mathematical properties allow propagation without dissipation. On a level different from that of mathematical analysis, several of the caravan felt gooseflesh rise.

"It's going to kill that bomber," said Peters, his voice flat. After so many personal deaths, the destruction of strangers had little weight.

The creature was dark at first, visible only in silhouette against the landscape, but its color changed as the particles within it began to rage. Hints of green and gold changed to violet. For an instant it became canary yellow in a flash of sodium luminescence. Then its entire form took on an orange and violent sheen.

"I've never seen one being born before," said Peters. "It's almost beautiful."

"So is a mushroom cloud," said Shreiber. "At a distance."

It sped after the B-52 and made short work of the aircraft. A few light touches and the wings took fire, aluminum alloy exploding into the searing incandescence of a thermite bomb. Then the plane exploded, the water cargo flashing into steam. The heat and reaction ripped the steam into its components and the hydrogen flare made a fireball that began to rise.

The creature leaped upon the hot blue cloud and merged with it, consumed it, swelled to four times its newborn size. Then the smoke plume from the hillside joined it and again black soot began to glow.

All who watched heard it but they did not know how the sound could reach so easily to the center of the head. They held their ears and tried to shield themselves from the scream of mockery, but there was no escape. It lingered, long enough for held breath to become painful. Eventually it subsided, as the creature began to rise and mutate once more. Eventually it gave a final, distant, laughing cry, and joined the dark smog clouds overhead.

"Was that my imagination?" Monica's voice cut through the diminishing static on the radio. "Or was that thing taunting us?"

"Maybe," Peters said into the microphone. "Like insults exchanged across the front line. It's got a sense of irony, too. Do you know what the name of the mountain is?"

"What?"

"Mount Olympus."

They reached the Hollywood house at about four A.M. They had had to leave the road twice during their journey, once to skirt an accident that had not been cleared away, the other to avoid a pocket of high concentration smog. Peters was heard to mutter something about modeling in complex terrain.

The computer terminal was already set up when

they arrived. Its green phosphor eye glowed balefully in the living room of the hillside house. Sliding glass doors connected the living room to the patio, which offered a view of the valley below. The glass bothered Peters, but he said nothing.

"Well, it's all ready," Monica announced to no one in particular. "'T'were well it were done quickly.'"

Peters nodded and sat down at the CRT. With sweating hands he typed: LOGIN MACGREGOR

The machine replied:
MACGREGOR LOGGED IN 14:49:34
PASSWORD: ⊗⊗⊗⊗⊗⊗⊗⊗⊗⊗⊗⊗⊗⊗
With sweating hands, he typed T-A-I-Y-O-K-A-M-U-R-I.

UFD TAIYOKAMURI OK
MACGREGOR (1) ENTRY PORT 142
SMOGMOD IV IN EXECUTION
NO SYSTEM MESSAGES

Everyone cheered but Peters's voice cut them off. "Quiet!" he yelled. "I'm glad that we're alive too, but we haven't solved anything yet. Joella, will you please get the recorder and our notebooks? Doug, Monica? Can you set up the Apple? We may need it to try some small-scale simulations or something. Everybody else just boil water or twiddle your thumbs. Somewhere else. I have a lot of work to do."

The explosions began just before dawn. A refinery complex in Long Beach was the first to go. Torrance quickly followed. Soon the coastline was ablaze. The fires burned slowly, with heat enough to melt steel; but the flames shed no light. The smog devils huddled about them.

Feeding.

The first rays of dawn touched the escape routes

from the city to show masses of wrecked and stalled vehicles. Roadcrews were attempting to clean up, to allow the tattered evacuation procedures to continue. It was not to be. Engines died. Tow trucks dissolved into slag. Men not fast enough to escape or unlucky or just stubborn, died gasping for air where suddenly there was none. Explosions racked the roadbeds, the passes, Newhall, the Grapevine. Interstate highways became broken rubble. The megalopolis was all but sealed off. The monster wanted no departures.

Tracking the thing was easy. The smogmod program outputs, the Execution Trace files, were everywhere. Tracks in the forest for a herd of devils, giant footprints for the father of them all.

It was also a somewhat disjointed record of the past few days. He had been right about the clean air episode. The transport algorithm parameters had been modified. This particular solution scheme, SHASTA, Sharp and Smooth Transport Algorithm, depended on a balance between numerical diffusion (for stability) and antidiffusion (to undo the effects of the numerical diffusion). But the antidiffusion step had been amplified and the chemical components of smog had been separated as effectively as if in a gas chromatograph. The monster had stored substance and grown fat.

Peters also located numerous examples of the "smog demons," the little submodels that allowed treatment of phenomena smaller than the resolution of the full grid. At first the demons had just been high concentration puffs of primary pollutants, hydrocarbons, nitrogen oxides, carbon monoxide, sulfur dioxide. Then some of the obvious secondaries had been amplified; ozone concentrations of a few thousand parts per million were indicated, hydrogen peroxide of ten to fifty percent.

Then it gained control of the unstable intermediates, the free radicals that drove the process. He found an indication of twenty parts per million of hydroperoxy radicals, a few PPM of hydroxyl and atomic oxygen. He gave a low whistle at that one. That wasn't smog anymore, that was combustion, a creature of living flame.

He found records of acid mists, of wind-driven dust that could probably cut through stone. He saw where and how the monster fed, the ways in which it digested its fare. He saw the records of the kills and the strange excitement that those events produced in the model.

He found the wind-shear episode that had killed his friends and colleagues.

EXECUTION TRACE: SMOGMOD IV
      LAGRANGIAN PUFF SUBMODEL

LOCATION: 40624.27,   1566.67   UTM   COOR-
DINATES
CELL (12.4 , 16.5)
          X   Y

TIME: 12.22

AVERAGE CONCENTRATIONS (PPM)

O_3	0.02
NO	****
NO_2	0.27
OLE	0.004
PAR	0.55
ETH	0.002
ARO	0.13
CO	22.4
PAN	86775.3
H_2O_2	265.0
HNO_2	****
HNO_3	***

```
RADICAL CONCENTRATIONS
O        2.1E-9    HO₂     5.3E-4    ACO₃    4.3E-2
O1d      3.6E-12   NO₃     1.OE-5    OH      1.7E-7
```

"That's a mother," he muttered.

"So's your old man," Ben replied, rolling his chair over for a better look. "What are we seeing?"

"High explosives, I think," Peters replied. "PAN, peroxyacetyl nitrate, is thermally unstable. I wouldn't have thought you could get a concentration that high, that's nearly ten percent. I'll bet that's what it's using to blow up the coast."

He typed:

```
FILIESPOOL LOCAL
DELETE TRACE
```

It answered:

```
ERROR
PROGRAM IN EXECUTION
INSUFFICIENT ACCESS RIGHTS
```

"Holy shit!" exclaimed Ben. "That's no trace file, that's a live program."

It was true. While they watched, concentrations changed. They were watching a smog demon in action.

"Can we hit it?" Ben asked. "Do something? That's what we're here for, right?"

"I don't know," said Peters, his breath tight in his chest. "Watch the windows."

He typed:

```
ADDON DATASET
SOLZENITH : : 9O(degrees)
EMISFILE
```

"Just trying to get your attention," he muttered. "Can I switch off the light or choke you on a big slug of NO_x?"

He tried another input modification. The numbers on the screen shifted again, then:

```
I/O ERROR LOGICAL UNIT 5
DISKREAD ERROR SYSB
PROGRAM ABORT
DUMPSPOOL TO ENTRY PORT
```

Then the screen went white with garbage symbols and the disk system on the local terminal emulator began to emit shrieking noises as it gouged lines into the floppy disk. Ben hit the power switch.

"You're not supposed to do that," Peters told him mildly.

"And it's not supposed to do *that*. What the hell happened?"

"I don't know about EPANET," Peters said, "but we have just demonstrated an ability to crash our own system. I think we took some hardware along with it. How soon can you get us booted back up?"

"We have enough spare systems here to start our own net. Maybe half an hour. I think I might be able to surge-protect the disk so this won't happen again."

"Great," Peters's voice was rich with sarcasm. "If the disk drive doesn't fall, maybe we can blow out the whole terminal."

"What about the smog devil? Did we kill it?"

Peters shrugged. "Maybe. So what? There's lots more where it came from."

Shreiber Manse

Arthur and Marty saw each other three times a day, during mealtimes back at Shreiber Manse. Each carried a tray upstairs, and Arthur would wait by the door, for safety's sake, while Marty gave the food to her ex-husband. But there was never any trouble.

"He just sits there, mostly," she told Arthur.

"Sometimes he smiles. Sometimes he winds up one of the toys and shows it to me, and then he smiles. That's maybe the spookiest . . ." She grimaced. "He's regressed to childhood or something. I wish we could get him some real help."

Arthur nodded. "When this is over, maybe . . ." He sighed. They were outside the door to Beth's room. He smiled at Marty. "See you later." Then he went inside to feed Beth.

She was never fully conscious, but managed a semidrowse to allow herself to be fed. At times she said things from her delirium.

"They're fighting," she said, when Arthur lifted her head.

"Who is?" he asked.

"White knights and a buncha clouds. Wait, no. Nights are black, right? So a white knight would be a day." She giggled.

"Here, have some soup," he said. She took it in her mouth and swallowed.

"No, but see, the knights are white and the clouds are black, but they're really all green, 'cause it's a CRT screen, a video. It's OK, though, they can fight 'cause it's all on TV." Suddenly, she sounded dubious. He gave her another mouthful of soup.

"Who's winning?" he asked, not really listening.

"Not a real fight," she said, slurring a bit, drifting back toward sleep. "Told you, it's all on TV. Clouds are too high and the knights' horses can't fly."

At first it had felt good, it felt like being on the offensive. He trailed it and stole information from it about its habits, how it worked on each of the planes that it inhabited. But there was never a direct encounter. He'd thought that Macgregor's login would put him in contact. But the monster was wily and treacherous. Surrogates he met aplenty. The little smog devils seemed to be all over the place. He attacked several, killed another one before it could escape. Others vanished when a section of the net crashed out on him. Further indication as to how *intrinsic* those things had gotten.

But he could not locate Big Daddy. SunSmoke itself was always six jumps ahead of him. So he found himself reduced to taking potshots at little baby smogs. Maybe he was even saving lives, out there in the real world. But it felt like playing the biggest computer game in the world and *he didn't like computer games*!

And there were walls in the forest. Secured parts of the system were off limits, or they took too long to crack. He couldn't get at the heart of it all. Macgregor had done it, but he couldn't get a glimmer as to how.

How?

The screen said:

PRIVILEGED ACCESS: ENTER SECURITY CODE
▓▓▓▓▓▓▓▓▓▓

It was not a sophisticated security system. It was probably part of some private system that was hooked into the net. Someone wanted to protect valuable files against accidental tampering. It took Peters and Ben nearly an hour to get in. They had to run through a few thousand probable access codes before they found the right one. Normally it wouldn't have been too difficult, but the system kept trying to log them off as they worked.

He left Ben at the console while he went to wash his face. Suddenly he found that he was shaking.

"Look," he told Shreiber. "When everything started, the main physical manifestations of the monster were mixing effects. Pollutants were being transported aloft and stored. Like a newborn baby,

SunSmoke was just eating and sleeping.

"Then certain chemical rate constants were modified. It eliminated its need for fresh nitrogen oxides by stopping the sink reactions. It reduced the reaction of the hydroxyl radical with NO_2, or it back-reacted nitric acid to yield nitrate radical.

"Part one was large-scale statistical, a modification of eddy diffusion. Part two changes statistical thermodynamics. Smaller scale, but more fundamental.

"Most recently, actual photolysis rates have been changed. The ability of compounds to absorb light has undergone some fundamental modification. That's quantum mechanics. What's next? Nuclear transformations? The creation of mass?"

Shreiber said, "Surely all that takes energy, power, effort of some sort."

Peters replied, "Maybe, but whose? There is some indication that it prefers the easier stuff. But it keeps testing the limits.

"Macgregor was using an adaptive program to do a parameter search. That's an AI protocol, pretty fancy. In fact, I thought the adaptive parameter scheme was one of the few encouraging aspects of artificial intelligence research. The program was going through its paces, trying to match up with the smog outside, when Macgregor died and somehow gave the program the power of life, or pseudolife or whatever damn thing you want to call it.

"The key thing is that parameter search routine. It's adaptive. The smog monster is slowly shaking itself free of limitations. I don't know what will happen then. We'd better pull the plug on this thing fast."

Just then Ben got up from the terminal and announced, "Lost it, folks."

The trail had been fresh. They had been analyzing

the process where the concentrations of peroxyacyl nitrates and other unstable compounds were pushed up in concentration until explosive levels were reached. The traces were only a few minutes old.

"And then it dived behind part of some system with major security. I think it's EPANET operating system security. It asked me my business, the watchdog system did, and then kicked me out. SunSmoke seems to be able to ignore that kind of thing, but we can't. So it can cut and run whenever we get close. Or maybe just bash us with a brick from behind a wall."

"So now what?"

"Beats me." Ben replied. "I think we need help. The system is well protected. It's distributed and there are a lot of different control points. But I think we're going to have to crack the security of the whole system and I have no idea how it can be done."

Shura

There was a place above and a place below. Below was structure, limitation, form texture, enclosed spaces. Boxes within boxes. If the *shura* could know humor it would have laughed at the petty scuffles down below.

Above was formless, alight with colorless sparks and the power of the air and light. The *shura* ruled this space and through the laws of this space it changed the nature of the land below.

Other beings lived in the void above, but they were unaware and therefore impotent. The *shura* manipulated them with careless ease. Below, there was awareness; at the lower levels there was conflict, but the spaces were too confined. The others could not move against the *shura*. They fought dreams, wisps, shadows. They tilted at the wind.

It did not know humor. But its laughter echoed through the shadows all the same.

It was not a dream. He was too tired, too agitated to sleep. But the image came to him with the force of a nightmare.

He saw Macgregor, standing, wide horse stance, close to the ground, punching a brick wall. His hands bled but he was oblivious. The blood mixed with the brick dust to make a nasty red paste that smeared equally on his hands and the wall. The wall was massive, immovable, yet it shook with each blow, and the small cracks grew larger and the mortar crumbled a bit more. With each blow the mortar crumbled a bit more.

Macgregor's breath came in deep, explosive gasps. The whole world shook when he struck.

The wall fell. It buried Macgregor in the rubble of its collapse. But from the swirling dust, there coalesced a creature of flame and acid with hot eyes that gazed out on the world with hatred and determination.

They were Macgregor's eyes.

Gary Huntington, Jr.

Gary Huntington, Jr., was a computer nerd. There was no other word for him. In college, he had taken to programming with the zealotry of a religious convert. He loved every part of the process, from the first flowchart to the final debugging. And he was good at it. Upon moving to San Francisco Bay after graduation, he had fit into the Silicon Valley scene as if born to it.

Almost everything about him said *programmer*.
His socks were often mismatched, and he never wore
ties. He wore a plastic pen holder in his shirt pocket
to protect his shirt from leaking ink. In his one con-
cession so far to west coast fashions, his shirts were
no longer white nylon, but gaudy prints.

Physically he was built a little like a duckpin,
narrow-shouldered and broad-hipped. He owned a
set of contact lenses, but preferred to wear glasses.

If Gary Huntington, Jr., could be said to have
troubles, they concerned his wife. Not that he didn't
love her; in fact he doted on her. They were much
alike. Apart from being similar in physical appearance, they had similar interests. They had met at a
Star Trek convention. Both read large quantities of
science fiction and fantasy. Both belonged to the Society for Creative Anachronism.

The problem at the moment was money, or lack of
it. Gary was well paid, but they had just bought a
house. Now his wife's birthday was approaching and
he wanted to buy her a nice present.

The ideal gift would be a word processor. She
wanted to be a writer and although she hadn't published anything yet, Gary enjoyed her work and
thought she had a lot of talent. What better gift than
a replacement for her old electric typewriter? But
word processors were expensive, so it came back to
money again.

But then, in the middle of a mild no-money grouse:

"Hey, sport, you used to work for EPANET,
didn't you?" The fellow addressing Gary was a bit
obnoxious, but then most of them were, weren't
they?

"A little, why? I used to have a part-time job for a
teacher who had some system development contracts
with them."

"Well then, you are sitting pretty. I heard it on the
QT, in fact it's probably conspiracy to even mention

it, but you should check out the Number Three Jolly Roger bulletin board.''

"Yeah?" Huntington knew the best way to wheedle this guy was to look dubious, instead of excited, which he was.

"Yeah. Five to fifty K, I believe, dollars not bytes. For information about Security and Systems Operations on the EPANET.''

"Well, I do know a bit about the master system. Getting to it is a bitch though. It's so well distributed that it only goes a piece at a time. And all the different command points have different security, 'cause they're on different machines."

"Even so, I'll bet they take what you've got."

"Maybe I'll look into it." Gary ambled away.

It took him about five minutes to get to a terminal and about fifteen to find out what was up. He even made a good guess as to who was doing it. Doug Shreiber was a legendary reprobate. With money. He hoped it was Shreiber. That meant it wasn't a hoax and the check wouldn't bounce.

But wasn't Shreiber still in L.A.?

He would have thought that people in L.A. would have plenty on their minds right now without making outlandish bets, what with the smog and all. But who was he to argue with an eccentric millionaire?

So Gary Huntington, Jr., sat down at his terminal and began to work. The sudden intensity of his concentration was awesome; he always worked as if his life depended on it. Maybe this time it did.

Walter and Joella

"I can't do it," he said dully. "It's impossible."

Joella looked at him coolly. "Raymond did it."

He managed to glare at her. "Raymond was insane. He was a maniac, tied into powers . . ." He groped for words. ". . . powers far beyond those of mortal men."

She fixed him with a look that he found terrifying. He could not escape it even by looking away or closing his eyes.

"You are stubborn," she stated. "Your determination is a match for Raymond's. You could do this thing; it is within you. Ray had no monopoly on magic."

He ceased trying to avoid her gaze.

"Maybe," he said. "But it would kill me just like it killed Ray. I don't know if I can do that. I'm not sure that I should. It's not . . ." His voice trailed off.

"It's not your way," she agreed. She kissed him lightly and brushed his cheek.

"You're tired," she said. "Come to bed."

Doug and Monica

"Doug?"

"Yes, Monica?"

"Are you awake?"

"Only for you, Monica."

"Don't make fun of me, Doug. The way I feel now, I'll either cry or kick you in the ribs. I'm scared."

"Should I turn on the light?"

"No, that doesn't help. The dark seems safer. That's right, isn't it? Photochemistry? It's a creature of light. It's stronger in the light?"

"Perhaps. It's also a creature of imagination. Maybe scrunching under the covers would help."

"Are you making fun of me again?"

"I don't know."

Silence, then.

"Can he do it?"

"I hope so. I think so. I don't know. Do what?"

"Damn you, you're trying to distract me. Can he find a way to kill SunSmoke?"

"If anyone can. If we're right, and I think we've reached the point where we're either right or crazy. If we're right, then this is some sort of symbolic personal combat. It has to follow a certain form, like a fairy tale, or a myth. Walter's the only person who can wear the magic armor. He's our champion, the only one we've got . . ."

"So?"

"So what?"

"My question dammit. So can he do it?"

Shreiber said nothing for a long time. Long enough for Monica to want to scream. Then he spoke.

"I taught one course with both Walter and Ray Macgregor. I remember Walter because that was where he came to my attention. There was an odd little incident; Macgregor had a part in it.

"The course was Computing Algorithms and Automata Theory. It was a mishmash. Math majors took it, engineers took it; it taught everything from numerical methods to computability theorems.

"With so many different kinds of students and so much material it was hard to grade. I couldn't tell who was getting what out of it. I thought it unreasonable to expect a biophysicist to get the same kind of insight that would be expected of a topologist. But I wanted to know what kind of insight each was getting and who was capable of what.

"Around midterm I had a test, take-home with some fairly knotty problems on it, many from areas we hadn't covered. I sort of threw them all off the deep end to see which ones could swim.

"One of the problems was totally unfair, something of a trick. It was a cleverly disguised example of a class of problems that are known as NP-complete. They are probably incomputable in finite time, so the problem as stated could not be solved. I wanted to see how clever the attempts would be and I wanted to see if anyone recognized the trap.

"Two of them did. Ray Macgregor turned in a twenty page proof showing the problem to be NP-complete with a few other things about NP-complete problems thrown in for good measure. It was a top-rate piece of work even if he had mostly cribbed from math journals and textbooks.

"Walter, on the other hand, turned in a single sheet of paper that said, 'I think I smell a traveling salesman.' The traveling salesman problem is a famous example of an NP-complete problem. Then he added a few lines, out of context, from a traveling salesman joke. The punchline was something about a nine-inch stump, I think."

Monica turned restlessly. "Yeah. Walter says he got pretty weird toward the end of his school days."

"As I did. That was just about the time I was setting up the Manse and realizing that having a lot of money meant that I didn't have to teach if I didn't want to, and I didn't want to. I bailed out next quarter, Walter the next year."

"So what's the point?"

"Eh? Oh. The point is, I gave both of them full credit. I couldn't think of anything else to do, or really, anything else that I wanted to do. Macgregor put in more work, but hell, anybody can put in time. Walter had done the difficult part, he had confronted the problem, he knew how to finish it. But he didn't want to jump through a hoop and I couldn't fault him for that.

"It must have really pissed off Macgregor, though, for Walter to do it like that and get away with it. Macgregor was like that. He knew how to do it right. If you didn't do it his way, then that couldn't be right; it must be wrong. Q.E.D. Walters always had the commendable attitude that there was more than one way to skin a cat. I liked his style.''

"And . . .''

"And the problem of cracking the security codes in the EPANET is in many ways like an NP-complete problem. Hell, it almost certainly *is* NP-complete. Macgregor somehow solved it, or got around it. Maybe. Hell, I don't know.''

"But Walter is . . .''

"Walter is trying to solve the problem like Macgregor did. That's not his style. But I can't sit him down in the chair and say, 'Dammit, think like Walter Peters, not Ray Macgregor.' I don't even know what that means. So we just have to wait. It's up to him, we're just the goddam cheering section. I think he can do it, but it's just blind faith.''

Silence stretching for a long time. A slow melting together in the dark.

"Doug?''

"Yes, I know. I'm scared too.''

Sleep

Joella led Peters upstairs and undressed him and stretched him out on the bed. Then she rubbed him with an aromatic oil, feet, legs, torso, neck and shoulders. After a while, his skin felt warm, almost glowing.

She massaged his scalp and he slowly began to drift into sleep as her hands shifted, moving lower on his body. But whenever he was just ready to drift off, she'd hit a knot of painfully tense muscles in his back or hips and he'd jolt into semiconsciousness. Then, slowly, the aching muscles would relax and join their warmth to the radiant glow he felt surrounding him.

His ears buzzed with her whispered words; he could not make out what she said.

Sleep claimed him, a gentle drifting fall into the light.

The dust motes danced in the sun streaming in through the saloon door. He wanted a drink, for courage, because his hands shook but he didn't dare. High noon was only an hour away and he had to meet Kid Shura then, he wasn't sure just why. It didn't seem right somehow, or even fair, what with Kid Shura being already dead and all.

He shook his head, in self-pity. "I don't think I can do it," he told the others. "He's so fast. He's got circuits for nerves and a silicon heart. Those micro-chip bastards are *small*! How can I hit something that size? And then there's the part of him being already dead and all."

Across from him sat Matt Dillon, not the TV version, but the one from radio, bigger, with a deeper voice. He couldn't quite see the Marshall's face but the voice was clear enough.

"You've got to show some gumption, boy. You'll never make black belt otherwise."

"But how do you kill a dead man?"

"With life," the Marshall said. "Here, these will help."

Dillon placed three bullets on the table and they all had silly grinning oriental faces carved on them. "That's ridiculous," he told the Marshall. "Those are just ridiculous."

"You think magic has to be solemn? That notion'll kill you for sure."

"But . . ." he said dubiously, "these are magic bullets? What magic have you ever done?"

The star of SunSmoke laughed out loud. In that laugh, his voice changed in character, but it was still recognizably the same. He called out over Peters's shoulder to somebody in the corner.

"Hey Rocky, watch me pull a rabbit out of my hat!"

"Again?" came the reply.

Peters turned with a start to see a cartoon squirrel with aviator goggles and cap. And when he turned back, the Marshall had taken off his hat to reveal cartoon antlers and a goofy expression.

"Nothin' up m' sleeve," the moose said as he ripped it off.

"Presto!"

From the hat he pulled a huge reptilian head, Godzilla, snarling and breathing fire. Marshall Bullwinkle grinned at Peters, shoved Godzilla's head back into the hat and held it out toward Peters.

"We're counting on you, son." And with that he took the three bullets from the table and tossed them into the air.

"One!" The first bullet went into the hat.

"Two!" The voice was different, a woman's maybe, like Joella's. The second bullet followed its brother into the hat. Then there was a long pause, the third bullet hit Peters on the head and bounced into the hat.

"Three." And it was his own voice.

Peters awoke with a start, his scalp tingling from where the dream bullet had landed. But he didn't notice.

He had the answer.

Turncoat

Rigeman was not sure that he even remembered what sleep felt like. Certainly he couldn't remember the last time he had slept. The closest that he could recall was a few catnaps (read: sudden collapse into oblivion) followed by sudden awareness of being half-dressed and hanging on to the engine heading for another fire.

The coast was completely out of control. They had abandoned it. They practiced triage and tried to contain the worst of it. But they were losing and they knew it.

"Dammit, Benjamin, hang onto it!" The hose had given a jolt and nearly slipped out of his partner's hands. What a miracle that the water pressure was holding.

"Oh God," croaked Benjamin. "It's another one."

Rigeman's hands nearly slipped at that one. He looked to the sky and saw that the other man was right. One of the smog devils was gorging itself on the flames and eyeing the truck.

"Turn your hoses on it! Quick! Pepper! Concepción! Wet down the truck!"

Not that it would do any good. It was too close and water didn't help. He knew only three guys that had seen one of them this close. And lived. He knew plenty of other guys who had seen it that close. Used to know anyway.

It dived at them and Rodriguez hit it with a blast of CO_2 from a canister on the truck. That and the hose streams erupting into steam seemed to jolt it a bit. It veered off, recondensed and came in for another pass. Rigeman wondered if he had time to throw up.

But the screaming roar of the creature cut off in midnote. Its entire body blew up like an exploding flashbulb, blinding the entire crew. Suddenly, the rush of water through the hoses seemed like deafening silence.

"What the fuck?" he heard Benjamin mutter. "What the fuck was that?"

Rigeman blinked at the green afterimage before his eyes. "You wanta ask questions, or you wanta fight a fire?" he asked in what he knew was a cheap imitation of bravado. But hell, the real thing would be back. He was still alive.

He blinked again. Damn funny afterimage though. Didn't look like the creature at all. Looked like some kinda dinosaur or something. Green and scaly. Kinda funny.

Hollywood Hills

When Monica and Shreiber came down early the next morning, the first thing they saw was the blackboard, covered with the notation that Shreiber and Joella had devised for the description of process magic. Above the hastily scrawled symbols were three lines of text:

NOW THAT'S WHAT I CALL A MESSAGE

and

THE MEDIUM IS A MASSAGE

Beneath that in a different hand:

THE MEDIUM IS A MASSEUSE

Joella and Peters conversed in hurried whispers as much as if afraid of breaking a spell of creation as fear of waking the household. But they looked up in unison at Doug's and Monica's entrance.

"Hi there," said Peters. "Let's talk about reality."

Peters got up and began to erase one of the blackboards. Monica and Shreiber pulled chairs over beside Joella and sat down. Peters turned and grinned slyly.

" 'Today's lecture is mighty important. Remember . . .' " He chuckled. "Sorry. I haven't really gone off the deep end, but I seem to be higher than a kite, so bear with me. The lecture won't be too long." He turned and drew a few diagrams.

"SunSmoke is a living creature with three aspects. He is a smog cloud, a computer program, and a magical entity that lives wherever it is that souls reside. We can't really know what that is or where it is, but we can sense and perceive him on that level because, well, hell, we live there too. In any case, we have to assault him on all three levels."

Shreiber scowled. "How can we assault him physically? The smog is so . . . big. How can you fight the air?"

Peters shrugged. "I misspoke a little. Actually, the beast is at more or less continual physical risk. He fights the ordinary workings of the weather, for example. The winds should blow him away. But they are deflected because of his control at a very abstract level. A pressure front is even more destabilizing. He's shrugged off the passage of two mild frontal systems since this all began. There's another on the way, and one after that; they queue up in the Pacific pretty regular. So if we can hit him solidly on the symbolic levels, the weather should take care of its part of the bargain."

"So how about pulling the plug on the computer?" asked Monica.

"I wish it were *that* easy. But there's no plug to pull. The EPANET is spread out over the entire country. Killing that many computers all at once is tricky—no, make that impossible. Too many plugs and who'd believe us? No, we need to crash the whole system, which we can do, provided we can get system access at the same level that SunSmoke has. I have Ben at work putting together the system-killer artillery. The grapevine came through pretty well on that and, Doug, you're going to have to be generous, I think."

"Happy to. Provided we live through this. But

that still leaves the hard part. Getting into the system at the command level. Do you have a handle on that one? Can you do it?"

Peters smiled. "I already have. Or rather, I realized that I don't have to. Macgregor already did it, why do it again? The little smog devils can penetrate the system to rejoin the parent. This morning I hijacked one of them. I have him in a cage."

Peters walked over to the terminal and turned up the brightness on the CRT. The pentagram glowed amber, a jagged sleepy eye. Inside it was . . . something. It hurt to look at it. Peters turned down the brightness.

"How the hell did you do that?" asked Monica.

"I gave it a new name. He's now named Godzilla." Peters began to write on the blackboard.

"The Godzilla program is like a bacteriophage. It will be able to penetrate the system because the system will recognize it as having access. Its outer shell is an access code. But inside, he's one of ours."

Joella rose and walked to Peters's side. "Do you see it? That is where its magic lies. SunSmoke is Taiyokamuri, a technological monster. He does not just remind us of a Japanese monster movie. He *is* a Japanese monster movie. He comes from the same place as Godzilla, Mothra, and Rodan. Hiroshima and Nagasaki were destroyed and a new terror entered into human consciousness. The culmination of the terror that H. G. Wells foresaw in *War of the Worlds.*"

Peters indicated a line of symbols, the weird blend of psychology and tensor calculus that they had devised for describing magic and the collective unconscious. "So death and terror spawn more death and terror. They are themselves alive. But other forces work to soften the spell. Life tries to grow from the death. So Godzilla starts off as a monster, destroying Tokyo, and as time goes by he becomes a savior, protecting Japan from other monsters.''

Joella indicated another line of symbols. ''So the essence of Godzilla, the truth of him, has power that can stand against SunSmoke. We need to awaken that power.''

''How do we do that?'' asked Shreiber.

Joella continued, ''Raymond died, and in his death he worked a spell of death. We must work a counterspell of life. We need a symbol of life, an innocent conduit into the myths that surround the beast. Youth, innocence, a heroic archetype in tune with Japanese and American mythology, contemporary mythology.

''Monica, you're the closest we have to a Japanese expert. How deep is the archetype of the boy-hero in Japanese myth?''

Monica's jaw dropped. She started to laugh. Peters looked at her and caught the laughter, like a contagion. Soon the two of them were in tears. Peters could barely stand.

''Would you mind telling us what's so funny?'' Shreiber asked.

''Oh, have I got a boy for you!'' Monica choked out and let the laughter escape from her again. Peters sat down beside her.

''There's a boy at the *dojo* . . .'' Peters said.

''His name is Hirotomi,'' said Monica. ''We call him Hero for short.''

The Valley of the Shadow of Death

A yellow diesel station wagon slowly descended into Glendale. A blue Audi followed close behind.

The air was breathable—just barely. It stank of dead things mixed with crude oil. The foul smells of pyridene and hydrogen sulfide assaulted the senses.

Eyes burned and throats became raw even through filter masks. The vegetation alongside the road shed leaves of dead yellow and brown.

Day became night as they descended. The opacity of the cloud overhead was total. The only light came from streetlights and the chemiluminescent glowering of the monster itself. The roads were deserted.

A few television and radio stations remained on the air. The official line held that the smog was in the final stages of burning itself out. Unusual weather conditions combined with freak accidents (or possible sabotage) had caused the destruction of the Los Angeles oil storage and refining industry. Smoke from the fires was expected to persist another few days.

"Crap," snorted Monica into her gas mask. "How much longer can they keep on top of the situation before people panic?"

"You can't riot in the streets when it hurts to breathe," said Peters. He switched to another radio station. Amazingly, it was a small religious station. They listened for several minutes to apocalyptic preachings interspersed with excerpts from the *Book of Relevations*.

"They're not too far off base," said Peters. "In the country of the crazed, the half-mad man is king."

"What do your colleagues think?" asked Monica. "Have any of the so-called experts hit on any good notions?"

"I'm not sure," said Peters. "I haven't heard from anyone for several days; I think that the 'proper authorities' are keeping everything under wraps. Besides, you know how dangerous it is to be poking your nose into this business. SunSmoke does not like to answer questions. I don't think there are many experts left."

"Do you think that there could be an element of revenge to it? The monster sprang from Raymond's psyche. Did he bear a grudge against many of his fellows?''

"Your guess is as good as mine, maybe better."

The walkie-talkie crackled. Shreiber was in the rear car with Joella. He announced, "Road block, people. Get out all your fancy IDs, Walter. We're going to have to do some fast talking."

Shreiber and Peters got out of the cars and walked over to the police car. Peters noticed that the official vehicle had solid rubber tires. Rough on the suspension, but they wouldn't rot as fast.

A police officer met them halfway. "Twenty-four hour curfew," he said through his ill-fitting gas mask. "Emergency business only."

"This is official business," said Peters. "I'm a researcher from upstate, liaison to the Air Resources Board. I'm supposed to pick up some air quality monitors from the Pasadena station." He handed over his ARB identification badge and various government laboratory IDs. The latter had no function but to allow him access to computing facilities, but he hoped that the policeman did not know that.

The officer scrutinized them carefully, comparing the photos with the man in front of him. He scowled. "You're supposed to notify the local PD if you have business in the area," he complained.

Peters shrugged. "Bureaucracy. Somebody was supposed to."

The man hesitated. "Well I guess it would be all right to . . ." He never completed the sentence.

Peters heard the shriek first. He whirled and dove to the ground, at the last instant turning his dive into a clumsy shoulder roll that carried him toward the station wagon. Both Shreiber and the policeman turned, startled, toward the direction of the noise.

The windows of the police car imploded with the first touch of the smog devil. The policeman inside managed to get one of the doors open before he collapsed, sliding to the ground with his feet still inside the car. As they watched, the paint on the car began to visibly peel and blister. The seals on the vehicle's fuel tank dissolved and there was an audible *whumph* as the devil sucked the gasoline into its form.

Monica and Joella both leaped from the cars, each carrying a metal fire extinguisher. Joella handed one to Peters, then reached back into the wagon for a third. Three billowing streams of white leaped toward the police car.

The smog devil shrieked again, but this time the cry sounded like a creature in pain. It rose into the air and advanced toward the station wagon. Monica yelled something in Japanese and hurled her extinguisher at it.

The explosion deafened them. The concussion mingled with the creature's last dying screech. One piece of metal shrapnel smashed into the roof of the police car, but otherwise the remnants of the canister found no mark.

Both Shreiber and the policeman had been driven to the ground by the blast. The policeman arose clumsily. "Harry?" he said to his fellow officer. He stumbled toward the ruined police vehicle. He knelt beside his stricken partner and began to cry.

Glendale General

When is an emergency room not an emergency room? When it's a whole hospital. When is a hospital not a hospital? When it's a madhouse.

The roads leading to the medical center were jammed with hulks, some of which could be recognized as having once been automobiles. Other masses were barely recognizable as having been metal. Twice they drove on surfaces that were not meant to be driven upon, sidewalk detours that jarred their unconscious passenger unmercifully. His partner, whose name was Whitley, gritted his teeth and tried not to show his agitation.

Peters, Joella, and Whitley had loaded the unfortunate Harry into the station wagon. "Take my car and get Hero," Joella told them. "That will be safer. Walter and I may be too much a risk; we may be drawing his attention. Let's not draw it to Hero. We'll meet you in Grifith Park on the way back."

"Shall we maintain radio silence?" inquired Shreiber.

"Just get Hero," Joella said in annoyance. "We have to get care for the policeman. We're responsible."

"What did you mean when you said that you were responsible?" Whitley asked after the two vehicles had parted. "And who's this 'he' you keep talking about?"

"Can we tell you later?" asked Peters. "The short version sounds too weird for you to be comfortable riding alone with us."

"Hey! Get that car out of here! Ambulances only!" An apparition waved a glowing baton. Amazingly, despite all the obstacles, there was still traffic of sorts near the hospital entrance. Joella gave her attention to the would-be traffic cop. He wore a respirator and a badge and precious little else. His skin seemed to be smeared with some sort of oil or ointment, presumably a protection from the smog. He looked like something from a body-builders book.

"We don't have time for this person," said Joella to Whitley. "He wants to flex his muscles and look important. It would take me too long to deal with him, so you'll have to do it. Use your badge *and* your gun."

Whitley took her meaning, not that he needed much encouragement. He reached out of the car window, grabbed the respirator, and hauled the man's head inside the car. Muscles' face was only a few inches from Whitley's chest.

"See that?" Whitley said in a snarl. "That's a real policeman's badge, just like real policemen wear. Not some jive-ass, slicked-up junior birdman, but the real *verismo*." His gun appeared in his other hand. "And this here is a real gun. You heard what I said about real policemen? My partner's in the back, he's hurt bad, and if you don't get the fuck out of the way, I'm going to blow a hole in you and call it resisting arrest! Now where the hell is the fastest way into this place?"

Muscles showed them the way. Quickly, for all the good that it did. They carried Harry on a makeshift stretcher (a blanket tied to two sticks) through the entrance littered with wheezing, moaning supplicants. A few tried to block their way, then melted away before the power of the badge. The intern on duty took one look at Harry and began to curse.

"Christ on a crutch, what happened to him?" Harry's hair was nearly white by this time, and blisters had formed on his skin. "Never mind, I don't want to know." He yelled into a walkie-talkie, trying to hear himself above the general uproar in the room. "Murray, how quick can we get somebody down here? I think we've got another lung shock."

The talkie spoke. The intern shook his head. "Dammit, not soon enough. How about if we send him up there? Okay, okay, I know. But it's a cop. There's another one with him, but he's okay. I'll send them . . . okay, if they can find it."

The intern turned to them. "Look," he said, "we've seen maybe a half dozen cases like your friend since this started. You've got to get him to the ICU immediately.

"Through the door. Up the stairs. Fifth floor. Don't try the elevator, it's too slow." He looked at

Whitley. "If anyone tries to stop you, don't stop."
Whitley nodded.

Peters looked at Joella. "Do we have time?" he
asked.

"No choice," she said. "We're responsible." They
picked up Harry and began to move.

Shock is one of the most aptly named maladies.
Despite the vast differences in the forms of initiation,
the general systematic response is the same, a malig-
nant lowering of blood pressure, constriction of
blood vessels to nonvital body parts (e.g., large
muscles, the skin), weak pulse, oxygen starvation
from suppressed respiration, death.

If the body can be viewed as a complex intercon-
nected system, exhibiting all of the characteristics of
such systems (nonlinearity, feedback, counterintui-
tive response), then shock is a characteristic response
to a sudden change of state outside of normal operating parameters. The most common trauma that human bodies are subject to, yet often cannot deal with,
include massive blood loss, injury to heart and lungs,
electric current, sudden extremes of cold and heat,
anaphalaxis, and toxemia.

The last three probably applied to Harry.

The early 1970s saw the first step toward the wed-
ding of systems engineering and medicine. Since
then, biomedical engineering had been a perpetually
hot item, generating much interest, but few practitioners, and several fortunate devices (e.g., CAT
scanners). But its potential remained largely un-
tapped, perhaps because of the natural antipathy between engineers and doctors.

Islands of cooperation existed and fortunately, the
unfortunate Harry wound up in one such place. The
trauma ward of Glendale General was a joint research project with Caltech, ideally suited to treat
someone suffering from a quick dip in hellfire.

"Yeah, he's not too far gone, we think," the intern told Whitley. "We've saved worse, just this week. Sometimes a trauma is so bad, the lungs and diaphragm turn to cardboard, then we have a hell of a time. But your friend seemed to stabilize okay. The respirator is one of our best; lucky for your partner the previous tenant croaked an hour ago. . . ."

"Are we done here?" Peters asked impatiently.

"Yeah, go ahead," said Whitley. "I'll stay here. I phoned in my report, and I sure don't need a ride back. We've abandoned that checkpoint."

Peters took Joella's arm and turned to go.

"Oh, uh, folks?" Whitley asked. "You said earlier something about . . . uh, I'll take the short explanation, no matter how crazy."

Peters couldn't help himself. "Okay," he said. "The smog is alive, controlled by a voodoo computer program that was written by a dead man who hates my guts. On the advice of Bullwinkle the Moose, we're on our way to get the hero of the story, a nine-year-old Japanese boy, who is the only one who can unleash our secret weapon, Godzilla, against the smog monster."

"Oh." There was not much Whitley could say to that. He'd been warned.

"Your partner is real lucky, you know," continued the intern. "In fires sometimes the lungs get scorched, and you get so much fluid in the lungs, from pneumonia or edema, that the patient often drowns. But it seems that people can't actually *breathe* enough of the smog stuff to cause that much damage . . ."

As they left, Peters whispered, "Talkative isn't he?"

"You would be too after forty-eight hours and a handful of speed. He gets it from the ambulance drivers, they usually have the best connections."

• • •

"Help me with this, would you? It's heavy and my back is trying to go out on me again."

A female intern was trying to balance a couple of carry-all baskets. Joella and Peters each took one.

"Thanks," the intern said. "This is real scut work, but if we waited for someone to deliver it, some of the asthmatics would go critical and I'd rather haul boxes than intubate wheezers. I'm supposed to be on call in neuro anyway."

They reached the asthmatic ward; the intern thanked them again and fled. Joella and Peters again found themselves drawn into a situation, loading syringes with epinephrine as the remaining intern moved around the room injecting each patient in turn. Then he made another slow pass around, listening with a stethoscope for the telltale sounds of breaking asthma, the bronchia dilating and loosened breath.

"It seems a bit stuffy in here," whispered Joella. She yawned mightily.

"Stuffy?" asked Peters. "Better than outside, I'd say," but he found himself yawning as well. "Dammit, that's contagious," he said. Joella said nothing. She yawned again, and stretched her body magnificently.

The intern could hardly help noticing her and was soon barely suppressing his own yawns. Suppressed yawns are at least as contagious as those left uncontained. Soon half the ward was in the grip of it. And the yawns were punctuated with little gasps of laughter, also contagious, also invigorating.

Arms stretched, spines straightened. A feeling of easyness and warmth passed through the room. Joella moved from patient to patient, touching forehead, neck, stomach, and chest. From time to time she would adjust the tilt of a head, slide the patient forward or back, whisper something in someone's ear that would bring a giggle and a sigh of relief.

The intern listened in wonder as in patient after patient breathing became regular and unforced, as the passageways to their lungs lost their constriction.

He stared at Joella. "How the hell did you do that?" he asked in a stage whisper.

"Magic?" she said innocently. "Faith-healing? Or how about this? The psychosomatic component of asthma has been reported to explain as much as sixty percent of the variance in onset of attack. Blood levels of epinephrine have been demonstrated to increase by as much as fifty percent with changes in posture alone. Smooth muscle relaxation and vascular dilation are both under a degree of hypothalmic control and can be strongly influenced by conditioned stimuli."

"Sounds like some kind of naturopathy to me," he began.

Suddenly the door swung open and a black head appeared. "Hey, Roy, I think we got a code!" the nurse yelled.

Roy rushed from the ward, followed by Peters and Joella.

The boy gasping for breath on the stretcher was about fifteen. He was nearly blue. Two quick hits of epinephrine did not obvious good. "Get a tube and a ventilator!" Roy yelled at one of the nurses.

"None left. The gaskets keep rotting."

"I . . ." Roy began. Then he focused on Joella. His eyes spoke.

Help me. Please. Help me. Help me; help him. I don't believe a bit of it, it's mumbo-jumbo but help me. If you've got some kind of magic, use it. Please. I don't want to watch another one die.

The stretcher was on the floor. Joella shoved Roy aside and lightly slapped the boy's face. His eyes focused on her.

"Hi," she said. "I think you're cute."

Her lips fastened on his and her cheeks puffed

slightly. Her hands caressed his legs, chest, stomach, and groin. She moved on top of him and their bodies began to writhe. The onlookers watched open-mouthed, too astonished to move.

"Lazarus come forth," Peters muttered to himself too quietly for anyone to hear. "Christ, Jo, if the Moose hadn't warned me against it, I'd say this was ridiculous."

It did not take too long for the sounds in the boy's throat to become something other than a gasping wheeze. Roy's face took on a look of fascinated embarrassment.

"Uh, she your girl friend?" he asked Peters.

"I hope so," Peters replied.

Roy shook his head. "You're a lucky guy . . . I think . . . you're going to need a lot of luck, you know?"

Peters said nothing.

Roy said, "Should we cover them up or something?"

As they were driving away Joella said, "I hope you're not mad."

Peters snorted, a bare inch away from hysterical laughter. "That was way too weird to get mad at. I'm just wondering what the hell happened."

She said, "Let's pretend that sometimes the body forgets how to do something vital. Like feel or think or breathe. Severe organic damage I can do nothing about. But if it's just the forgetting, if it has not progressed too far, it can be made right. Breathing especially is basic. There are many avenues to the doorway. I reminded those people of the rightness of their reflexes.

"Especially the boy."

"Mm. I think he'll remember correct breathing now. Single-step conditioning is difficult, but I think I effected a cure on that one."

"You know something, Joella?"

"What?"

"You talk funny."

"It goes with the territory, sweetheart."

"You know something else?"

"Yes?"

"I love you."

"I know."

Brief silence.

"Walter?"

"What?"

"I love you too."

"I know. Took us both long enough to admit it though, didn't it?"

Hollywood

They rejoined Monica and Shreiber at the entrance-way to Griffith Park. Another checkpoint, ominously deserted. Hero and Shirley were also in the station wagon.

Monica's fellow judo student Koichi had not been home; he had been on business outside of L.A. when the roads had closed and he was now trapped outside the city. His wife, Shirley, and Hero were home, however. It required little persuasion to get them to evacuate. Shirley called Koichi to tell him of their plans and he willingly gave his approval.

They made their way back up into the hills without incident. On the way, Monica told Shirley briefly of their need for Hero's help. Her glib explanation conveyed little in the way of real information; it left the impression that they needed someone with small hands to assist in the repairs of a computer.

When they arrived back at the "forward base," Ben was busy typing on the terminal connected to the

Godzilla program. "Couple of guys upstate had similar ideas about the EPANET," he said. "I've combined their programs into something to give Godzilla teeth and claws. It's a tapeworm program. The idea is to seek out memory dedicated to the Smogmod program and to pre-ëmpt it, to tie up as much of the net as possible. Some of the space involved is used for the EPANET systems routines, so there's a good chance that the whole net will crash."

Monica and Shirley adjourned to another room at Monica's insistence for some last-minute "packing." Shreiber, Peters, and Joella took Hero into the room that had been prepared for the spell-casting.

The walls were decorated with posters of Godzilla, in all of his cinematic glory. A song in praise of the monster, performed by Blue Oyster Cult, played on a portable stereo. The CRT sat in the middle of a pentagram, the five corners lit by sweet-smelling candles. Hero's face lit up in wonder and delight. "Hey, neat!" he said.

Peters smiled at the boy. It was impossible not to. Hero was a beautiful child, with a quiet broad face that became even broader when he smiled. Peters looked into Hero's dark brown eyes and sincerely hoped that what he was about to ask for wasn't dangerous.

"Well, it appears that we don't need your help in fixing anything after all. The machine is working and the program is ready to roll. You know what a computer program does, right?"

"It's the instructions that tell a computer how to solve a problem," the boy replied.

"Good. That's correct. Now the particular problem that we're working on is very difficult. It has to do with what's causing the smog that we've been having."

Hero grimaced. "Yeah, I know," said Peters. "We think it stinks too. We're trying to find ways to stop it, and this computer program is part of our research project. We've named the program Godzilla because we're going up against a smog monster."

"I saw that movie on televison," said Hero.

"Did you like it?"

"It was okay. I've seen better Godzilla movies, though."

"That's all right. We're just using Godzilla as our mascot, our good luck charm. We need all the luck that we can get, because the smog monster is a tough customer." The boy nodded.

"Tell you what," said Peters, his palms beginning to sweat. "We have the program all set up. All it needs is for someone to go over to the terminal and push the key marked RETURN. Would you like to set it off? Wish Godzilla a lucky time of it? We need all the luck that we can get, like I said, and I think that it would help if a Godzilla fan such as yourself were to do the honors."

Hero looked at Peters with the look that children give adults who are behaving in a childlike fashion. *Best to humor them*, the child perhaps was thinking. Who knows why grownups do anything?

So Hirotomi stepped over the chalklines and pressed the key marked RETURN.

"Go to it, Godzilla," he said. "You're the strongest one of all." The screen began to flash out the command sequence. The candles flickered and the lights dimmed as if from a power surge. The boy smiled at the special effects.

"Good luck, Godzilla," said Shreiber beneath his breath. "Give 'im hell."

In the equatorial Pacific sat a high pressure cell, slowly meandering with the motions of the sun.

The atmosphere is a turbulent heat engine, unpredictable in practice, perhaps unpredictable in principle. The energies of its motion flow from large-scale motions into small-scale eddies; the reverse is also true. It has been postulated that the flutter of a butterfly's wings can change the course of a thunderstorm.

So perhaps it was a butterfly's flight that was ultimately responsible for the high pressure cell's next action: it wobbled.

The wobble of a weather system in the Pacific has no direct connection with the weather to the north, but certain relationships between equatorial events and more northerly weathers do exist. Such relationships are known as teleconnections, but their predictive capabilities are slight. Only in the wintertime, when the atmospheric heat engine is at low throttle, do the teleconnections show up at statistically significant levels. Even then only a fraction of the variance of a season's weather can be explained. In summertime . . .

One high pressure system wobbled just as another cell began to collapse. A low pressure system, somewhat to the north, shrank a bit. A secondary eddy developed in an air mass farther to the west that would eventually become a monsoon. All was random happenstance. The sum total of these events was to nudge a high pressure region that sat much farther to the north: the Hawaiian high.

The high pressure ridge that sits over Hawaii is a more or less permanent fixture of Pacific meteorology. Its influence often extends as far as the west coast of the United States, shielding California from low pressure stormfronts during the summer, and assuring clear skies and smoggy weather.

In response to the nudge from the scattered air masses farther south, the Hawaiian high retreated just a bit. A gap appeared in the pressure ridge covering the west coast and into this gap moved a low pressure system.

The low pressure system was nearing the end of its

own tortured path from the lowly latitudes of the Pacific. It lurched toward the California coast.

Upon the coast of southern California crouched an air mass unlike any other on the face of the Earth. It was hot and stratified and quite unwilling to be moved by any outside force. Certainly it would take more than the gentle push of a low pressure front to move it. On two previous occasions it had turned such encounters aside.

This new low pressure front was somewhat more energetic than the previous systems. Perhaps it had more strength of will, although such a fancy is ridiculous on the face of it. Still . . .

Instead of altering its course in any horizontal direction, the low pressure front moved in the vertical. It began to climb.

The top of the smog system was intensely hot; drawing energy from the sunlight, the smog monster maintained an intense thermal gradient in its upper layer, effectively trapping all air below it. The low pressure system began to draw energy from the interface. Warm and moist, the air continued to rise.

As the air rose, it cooled. As it cooled, the moisture within it began to condense. The condensation released heat that kept the density of the newly formed cloud lower than the surrounding air. The cloud rose. Another phase transition began to occur. Ice crystals began to appear. The cloud continued to rise.

A great tower of air now surged high above the city of Los Angeles. Its upper reaches penetrated the stratosphere. It was a thunderhead of enormous proportions, far more powerful than the usual stormclouds that came to California. It was a creature of moisture and electricity. Its eyes were lightning and its breath was thunder.

Poised.

Waiting to attack.

Hollywood

They stood on the balcony watching the valley below. Shreiber asked Peters, "See anything?"

Peters looked upward, squinting. "I think so," he replied. "The weather reports say there's a front moving in; there may be a storm brewing. So our timing is pretty good. And is it my imagination, or is there a certain lumpiness developing in the smog cloud?"

Shreiber looked out, adjusting his eye-protecting goggles to get a better look at the dark masses of air. "Maybe," he conceded. "What does that mean?"

Peters gestured back toward the house. "We lost contact with the Smogmod program when we initiated Godzilla, so all I have is surmise. From the newscasts and police band monitoring, there seem to be fewer sightings of the individual smog demons. That could mean that he's consolidating them, reducing the amount of storage devoted to the Lagrangian subroutines that kept track of the demons. The lumpiness might mean that he's reducing the resolution of the overall grid structure. The fewer things that he has to keep track of, the more computationally stable the system will be."

"So what does it all mean?" asked Shreiber.

"It means that we have him worried," Peters said.

Shreiber Manse

Beth slept uneasily, but it was better than being awake. When she was awake, bright lights made her tremble and the everpresent stench of the smog seemed to cling and paw at her. Every movement seemed stifled and claustrophobic.

So she slept with the air conditioning turned up

full, with Arthur watching over her for those times when she would cry out and awaken wild-eyed and confused.

While she slept, she dreamed.

In her dreams were swirling waters, and seething fog which hovered just off the California coast. From the churning waters a form began to rise, reptilian and sentient. A creature come to carry out his appointed task.

What was his task? Godzilla turned his head as if to listen to a whispered plea. Oh, yes. Protect the children, that was his mission. Protect the children from all who would do them harm.

Astride the land there loomed a creature of mist and light. Taiyokamuri, SunSmoke, the smog monster. An alien beast conjured from a chemical hell, a creature bent on wanton carnage and destruction, enemy to Godzilla and all that he would protect.

Godzilla snarled a scaly snarl and arose from the swirling sea. The fog clung to him like a cloak.

With a roar Godzilla hurled himself upon Taiyokamuri. At first contact the lightning flashed and thunder mingled with the bellowed cry of Godzilla's anger. Lizard jaws tore a gout from the side of the smog monster, but the flesh turned to mist in Godzilla's jaws and the rent repaired itself in an instant.

The creatures grappled and lightning came again. The smog beast glowed with internal fire, misty talons raking at Godzilla's side. Godzilla bellowed again and smashed his foreleg into the glowing mass. Both creatures reeled. The smog beast recovered first and lashed out once again. Godzilla fell headlong into the coastal mud.

SunSmoke leaped upon the fallen reptile. The mist condensed, compacted, became dense and stifling. The smog beast enveloped Godzilla's head, intending to pin him down and choke Godzilla's life away.

But Godzilla is the strongest one of all! His bellow

lit his fiery breath and the gout of flame drove SunSmoke from his hold. Godzilla picked himself up and the lightning came to him; his form glowed with the power of it. He leaped upon his adversary. Both creatures fell amid lightning flares and quaking earth.

And there amid the rain and fire and chemical muck, the final scene began to play.

Monica adjusted her mask and stepped out onto the patio. A hot gust of wind tore at her, followed by a blast of icy mist that stung the skin as it evaporated. Shreiber turned to greet her.

"Are Shirley and Hero safe?" he asked her.

"I think so," she replied. "Donald just called to let me know that they've arrived. If that old bomb shelter isn't safe nothing is. How about this place? Isn't this patio just a bit exposed?"

He shrugged. "Safe as houses, I guess. We wanted to see the fruits of our labors, even if it killed us."

Lightning flashed and split a tree not a hundred yards from where they stood. The quartet ducked as a rain of splinters swept around them. Peters and Joella retreated behind an upended table. Shreiber sat down upon the damp concrete, trying to maintain an air of nonchalance.

"I waive simultaneous translation," he said.

Monica sat down beside him. They watched as the sky boiled.

The lightning flashes left phosphorescent trails of passage. The clouds shimmered with a thousand almost colors that hinted of sunlight and rainbows. The wind would shriek out its agony in one moment; in the next, there would be unearthly quiet. The accumulated and shifting smells in the wind had long ceased being identifiable. Another lightning bolt flashed, this time deep violet.

"I think I was in this movie," said Monica.

"How did it come out?" asked Peters.

"I don't know," she said. "It was a bit part and I died in the first reel. I couldn't stand to sit through it to the end."

EPANET SYSTEM MESSAGES 6/27/86

```
15:21:27   SYSB
      POINTER FAULT
      DISKWRITE ERROR:   RECOVERABLE
15:28:42   SYSG
      PARITY ERROR ACCESS PORT 129
15:31:12   SYSC
      POINTER FAULT
      NETWORK BUSY
15:36:58
      JOBNAME GDZLLA
      ACCESS VIOLATION
      ILLEGAL SEGMENT NUMBER
15:37:05   SYSA
      PARITY CHECK PHONELINE
      NETWORK BUSY
15:37:52
      JOBNAME SMGMDIV
      POINTER FAULT
15:38:35 SYSB
      DISKREAD ERROR:   RECOVERABLE
```

Dr. Jeffries was playing with his computer. Another man might try to rationalize his activities as work; he *was* running a kinetics program after all, and the data base he was linked to was for accessing technical journals. But his activities didn't really require the fancy graphics he was using and he sure as hell didn't have to make modifications to the operating system on his micro while he worked. He found it all interesting though, and he just liked to play with computers. So there.

He grinned. Maybe he could interface with the 3-D plotting routines to draw contour maps of ozone concentrations. Someone had once suggested that you could use a fast Fourier transform to . . .

The terminal emitted a blip and there appeared an error message he'd never seen before. Then it was replaced by a string of garbage symbols. He was hooked up to the data base through the EPANET system, so he queried the network OS. It spit more nonsense back at him so he jumped over to his own computer's watchdog system (he'd written it himself) and checked the status.

Then he watched helplessly as whatever garbage he'd hit in the EPANET gobbled up all his allocated memory, trashing his kinetics runs, students' grades and household accounts. Finally his whole system went dead, total gridlock, he'd have to boot it from scratch and who knows what all was lost?

Damn government computer system, he muttered. Couldn't it mind its own business and not piss on everybody?

```
15:39:10
     USER#   CX93
     FATAL ERROR–CONTACT SYSTEM
          ADMINISTRATOR
15:40:00   SYSB
     POINTER FAULT
     NETWORK BUSY
15:40:05
     JOBNAME GDZLLA
     DISKFULL
     SPOOL TO TAPE
     RELOAD
15:40:25   SYSE
     FILE TRUNCATED AND DELETED:   RECOVERABLE
```

15:40:41
    USER#   MY28
    MAXIMUM NUMBER OF PROCESSORS EXCEEDED
    YOUR PROCESS FORCELOGGED OFF: NOT
        RECOVERABLE
    CONTACT SYSTEMS ADMINISTRATOR
15:40:53
    JOBNAME SMGMDIV
    DISKWRITE ERROR: RECOVERABLE
15:41:12   SYSA
    ACCESS VIOLATION
    NOT LOCATABLE
15:41:20
    PHONELINE DOWN (213) 526-0517
    PHONELINE DOWN (213) 472-4011
    PHONELINE DOWN (213) 456-2153
    PHONELINE DOWN (213) 835-3527
    PHONELINE DOWN (213) 889-8979
    PHONELINE DOWN (213) 325-9375
15:41:40   SYSE
    DISKFULL
15:41:55 OPERATOR QUERY: WHAT HAPPENED IN
        SOUTHERN CA?
    ALL AREA CODE 213 PHONELINES JUST WENT
        OUT
15:42:07
    USER#   BE42
    ILLEGAL SEGMENT NUMBER
15:42:39 REPLY TO OPERATOR QUERY: NEWS SAYS
    SMOG, WEATHER FORECAST SAYS THUNDER-
    STORMS. MIGHT BE A QUAKE. WE ARE FIFTY
    MILES NORTH (LANCASTER) AND WE JUST FELT A
    JOLT
15:43:43
    JOBNAME SMGMDIV

```
MAXIMUM NUMBER OF PROCESSORS EXCEEDED
YOUR   PROCESS   FORCELOGGED   OUT–NOT
   RECOVERABLE
CONTACT SYSTEM ADMINISTRATOR
```

"Damn!"

The computer operator at NCAR (National Center for Atmospheric Research) had reason to swear. Disk crashes are a messy business and he had been just about ready to do a tape backup. Too late now; hours of work had just been trashed.

The jangling telephone nearly leaped into his hands. "Hello, Jeff?" he said into the mouthpiece. "Yeah, I was just about to call you. Complete wipe-out in disk drives at this end. I managed to isolate the vector pipeline machines, but we lost the EPANET lines entirely. I gotta run; I'll get back to you."

It was nearly two hours before he had the system up and stabilized. He then tried using the EPANET dial-up. There was no answer.

"That's funny," he said to himself. "Must be some problem with the phones."

```
EPANET SYSTEM MESSAGES   6/27/86
   15:44:06  SYSA  DOWN   NOT RECOVERABLE
   15:44:07  SYSB  DOWN   NOT RECOVERABLE
   15:44:08  SYSC  DOWN   NOT RECOVERABLE
   15:44:09  SYSE  DOWN   NOT RECOVERABLE
   15:44:10  SYSF  DOWN   NOT RECOVERABLE
   15:44:11  SYSG  DOWN   NOT RECOVERABLE
   15:44:12  SYSH  DOWN   NOT RECOVERABLE
                        •
                        •
                        •
```

Beth awoke to open windows and the sound of rain. Arthur was by her side. "Hi," she said weakly.

"You missed all the excitement," he told her.

"Excitement?"

He nodded. "Thunderstorm. Hail in some places. Tornado sightings. All capped off by the earthquake."

"I dreamed of an earthquake," she said.

"Well, it was no dream," Arthur told her. "Peters says that it may have helped kill the smog monster by taking out some of the telephone system and helping to crash the computer net. The rainstorm certainly helped."

"Could we go outside?" she asked.

"Sure," he said, and he picked her up and carried her out onto the balcony. The rain had turned to a fine mist.

"It's clean now," he said pointing to the rain. "It was pretty dirty at first. Almost black. But it killed the smog."

She shook her head and smiled. "It wasn't the rain," she insisted. " 'Twas Godzilla killed the beast."

Epilogue

For the June billing period, the California Air Pollution Research Institute received a bill for computer charges from EPANET for $746,629.66. The comptroller for CAPRI called the EPANET billing office the next day.

The comptroller for CAPRI pointed out that the charges were supposedly incurred under the account of Raymond Macgregor in the final three weeks of June. The comptroller also pointed out that Macgregor's accounts had been terminated with the discovery of his death on June 7 and that, therefore, the bill was in error.

EPANET billing was forced to agree with this conclusion. A new bill would be prepared and an apology would be forthcoming. The unprecedented EPANET system collapse of June 27 must have been responsible for the billing malfunction. Again our apologies.

Thus was another legend added to the apocrypha of the computer age: about how a computer sent a three-quarter of a million dollar computing bill to a dead man.

And in San Jose, Gary Huntington, Jr., purchased a word processor for his wife. She is currently working on a fantasy trilogy.

ACKNOWLEDGMENTS

I consider myself extraordinarily fortunate in having an outlet for those weird notions that come when one is in the midst of dealing with knotty problems (not all of them technical). Professionally, I am engaged in the simulation modeling of photochemical smog, about as arcane a subject as exists. There may be a dozen people with an equivalent job, maybe a hundred sufficiently familiar with the subject that we can converse. To be able to use this hermetic experience to write popular (I hope) fiction, is more pleasant than I can describe.

So, as if entering a contest for surreal eclecticism, I'd like to thank people who made significant contributions to this story. First and foremost, I acknowledge J. P. Lodge, editor of *Atmospheric Environment* and whose essay, "An Anecdotal History of Air Pollution," was a major catalyst and inspiration. No less important are my superior and colleague Dr. Gary Z. Whitten, from whom I have learned all the gas phase kinetics that I know, and Dr. Marcia Dodge, our contract monitor at EPA ORD whose financial and professional support has been essential in our research.

I also offer my thanks to all of my colleagues whom in various guises I have tortured, killed, and maimed so mercilessly in this book. I have shamelessly distorted and edited names, personalities, gender, professional station and standing, all in the name of fiction and good fun, and I didn't mean any of it, honest.

Special thanks are also due to Melissa Michaels and Sue Bennett who helped with the typing of the various versions of this fantasy.

Beyond that the list grows very diverse. So in no particular order I acknowledge:

Susanna Jacobson, Dave Stout, Sharon Farber, Sherry Gotlieb, William Conrad, Jay Ward, Dale Enzenbacher, Marty Cosper, Shawna McCarthy, Beth Meacham, Melissa Ann Singer, Randy Newman, Jim Morrison (RIP), Buck Dharma, Elizabeth Lynn, Amy Sefton, the entire Japanese monster movie and animation industry, Joyce and Aya Baptista, Ben Sano, John Howard, Koichi and Hirotomi Nii, Shirley Berg, Mike Liu, Shep Burton, Lynn Williams, Jacquin McIlvane, Maude Kirk, Larry Todd, Dorothy Smith, Charles Tart, Mikey Roessner-Herman, Terry and Carol Carr, Patrick Mason, Grant Canfield, Fritz Leiber (who should get an entire paragraph for *Our Lady of Darkness*), Doug Albert, Leon Martell (for *Billy Chops Bricks*), and the rest of Duck's Breath Mystery Theater, Barry Baumen, Alan Vincent and his wife Kathy, Jim Nagy (RIP), James P. Killus, Sr., and his wife Sue (Hi, Mom!), Murry and Ann Drescher, and last but not least, Cindy, the beer, and the comfy chairs at Shattuck Avenue Spats, where I finished this up, under the gun and on the run after eighteen months of living dangerously, thank you all so very much.

ACE
SCIENCE FICTION
SPECIALS

Under the brilliant editorship of Terry Carr, the award-winning <u>Ace Science Fiction Specials</u> were <u>the</u> imprint for literate, quality sf.

Now, once again under the leadership of Terry Carr, <u>The New Ace SF Specials</u> have been created to seek out the talents and titles that will lead science fiction into the 21st Century.

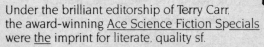

__ THE WILD SHORE Kim Stanley Robinson	88871-2/$2.95	
__ GREEN EYES Lucius Shepard	30274-2/$2.95	
__ NEUROMANCER William Gibson	56957-9/$2.95	
__ PALIMPSESTS Carter Scholz and Glenn Harcourt	65065-1/$2.95	
__ THEM BONES Howard Waldrop	80557-4/$2.95	
__ IN THE DRIFT Michael Swanwick	35869-1/$2.95	

Prices may be slightly higher in Canada